THE MASTER OF MAGIC

JAMES E WISHER

SAND HILL PUBLISHING

CHAPTER 1

Summer had finally arrived in the new empire and Otto was thoroughly enjoying the warm weather. Nearly freezing to death in Straken had given him a greater appreciation for heat. And speaking of heat, Villares had been turning it up on the southern border.

The former king of Rolan was now a bandit lord. His forces had struck half a dozen times across the border, hitting small villages and a caravan that decided to try and trade with Rolan despite repeated warnings and the unsettled climate. Happily, that had been a caravan run by a Franken competitor, so Otto's family suffered no loss. Not that Otto could simply let matters stand. An attack on any Garenland merchant was an insult that couldn't be allowed to go unanswered.

Which was why he found himself once again riding south on a hard wagon seat beside Hans. At least the wagon didn't bounce much with the heavy armor in the bed. The rest of the squad was behind them in their own wagons. Otto didn't know how much use the magical suits of armor would be in a fight on the open plains, but he felt better having them along.

The guys were all back in their official uniforms and mail armor. There was no point in pretending to be mercenaries now.

The small group was joined by Oskar, the Rolan infiltrator; Corina, the skinny girl that appeared stuck to him; and ten Rolan wizards eager to repay Villares for his treatment of their families. Five thousand spearmen taken from the Southern Army, along with all their supplies and followers, were somewhere behind the main group. Otto didn't expect to encounter a large force until they crossed the border. When that happened, the group would be forced to travel at the pace of the infantry.

"There it is, my lord." Hans pointed at a small town on the horizon.

Otto grimaced. Grunewald, once Garenland's southernmost village and now the invaders' base. Since the raids had resumed, Otto felt no guilt in slaughtering every Rolan soldier in the place. Well, maybe not all of them, he'd need a few to question. The trick was going to be doing it without killing their own citizens. Today, burning the whole village to the ground wasn't an option. Pity really, fire could only improve the miserable place.

"Don't get too close," Otto said. "I want to have a look around before we go in."

Hans pulled into a clearing just off the road. There was barely enough room for all five wagons. As soon as they stopped, Otto extended his sight towards the village. He'd scarcely reached the edge of town when Corina asked, "What are you doing? I can see a long line of ether stretching from your eyes."

"Forgive me, Lord Shenk," Oskar said. "She came over before I could stop her."

"It's fine," Otto said. He found he liked the girl's curiosity. It reminded him of himself when he began his journey as a wizard. "I've extended my sight through the ether so I can see what's happening in the village. Be quiet for a moment while I look around."

The girl obliged, allowing him to spy in peace. She was a clever girl, always eager to learn. She also knew enough to obey his orders. He didn't mind giving her pointers, but there was a time and place for instruction and this wasn't it.

Focusing on his task, Otto looked around the village. Nothing much had changed since his last visit. The buildings were still run down, the people outside still sullen and scowling. More Rolan soldiers clustered on street corners and now they wore their brown uniforms. Seeing as how everyone knew they ruled the village, there probably wasn't much point pretending.

Otto went straight for the stone building Captain Mendelson called his headquarters. Slipping through the stone walls, Otto found the man himself and half a dozen officers gathered around a map of Rolan and Garenland. There were some marks he didn't recognize, but given the position of the ones in Garenland, he assumed they were indicating where recent battles had taken place. If there was more intelligence to be gathered, Otto wanted it all.

And the only way he was going to get it was to sneak in and take Mendelson by surprise.

Otto blinked and returned his sight to his body. "We'll go in tonight. Let's find somewhere to hide the wagons."

On the plains, their options were limited. The best they could do was a swale a quarter mile off the road. Combined with the wizards creating an illusion to hide their tracks, it should suffice until sunset.

A camp chair gave Otto a modicum of comfort as he settled in to wait. He'd barely sat when Corina came over and joined him. "How about another lesson?"

"Didn't one of the Rolan wizards offer to teach you the basics?"

"Yes, but I don't like the way he looks at me. I've caught him staring at my chest twice when he thought I wasn't paying attention." She shuddered.

Otto couldn't imagine why anyone would want to stare at her flat chest, but whatever. He didn't have anything better to do until the sun set. "Have you managed a solid thread yet?"

She held out her hand and a wavering, indistinct thread of ether formed above her palm. Corina's thin face scrunched up in concentration as she made it thicker and more solid.

At last she blew out a long breath and the thread vanished. "That's the best I can do."

Otto shook his head. "Still too thin. You need to make it about twice as thick if you want to accomplish anything. Just keep practicing, you'll get there."

She glowered at him. "I've been practicing for months and I can't even manage a single spell. How am I supposed to fight like this?"

"I trained for two years under a dedicated master, six days a week, before I could conjure a usable thread. Now I'll grant you that my master was deliberately trying to hold me back and I was only eight years old at the time, but even so, mastering magic is a time-intensive thing. At the beginning, even the simplest task will exhaust you in seconds. It's no different from learning any new skill. You wouldn't expect to fight a duel after only a few months of sword training, would you?"

"Of course not, it's just frustrating. I want to help hunt down King Villares and if I can't use magic, what use am I?"

Otto didn't have a good answer for her. If he was being honest, he would have gladly left her behind with Master Enoch to teach her. She had come with Oskar to the capital so he could make a report before they began the invasion. When she found out a mission to hunt down Villares was setting out, she'd shown up and joined them at the portal. He understood how she was feeling and didn't send her away. Perhaps seeing Villares lose his head would help her accept the death of her parents.

As for her being useful in the hunt, there were plenty of things people wanted to do that they weren't capable of doing. Despite his best efforts, Otto had reached a ceiling in his own training. He kept pushing, but much like when he reached his personal limit, he was having trouble breaking through.

That wouldn't stop him from continuing to train, but it was frustrating.

"You just have to do your best, the same as the rest of us."

After the sun set, Otto waited another hour before standing and stretching. It was a clear night and the stars were bright. There should be plenty of light for them to make the hike to Grunewald. A faint hint of smoke perfumed the air. Everyone was probably at the dinner table, which made it a perfect time to strike.

"Hans, you and your men are with me. The rest of the wizards will surround the town and act as backup. Oskar, you and Corina will remain here. If this goes badly, you need to alert Wolfric to what happened."

"I think I'd rather risk capture than have to tell the emperor that his chief advisor has been captured or killed," Oskar said.

"I want to go too," Corina added.

Otto scrubbed a hand across his face. Bad enough General Varchi questioned his every decision, now these two as well?

"We're not having a debate. I'm telling you what's going to happen. Corina, remember that discussion we had earlier? If there's a fight, with your current skill level, you'll be in the way. Don't worry, your time will come. Oskar, so help me if she sneaks away and follows us, I'll nail you to the Garen city wall. Clear?"

Oskar nodded. "Perfectly, my lord."

Corina looked away and pouted. Was she really only two years younger than him? Otto hoped he'd never been that petulant. Not that he planned to ask his mother about it; he doubted he'd like the answer.

"Let's go." Otto enhanced his vision and set out toward Grunewald.

They reached the base of the wall half an hour later. As barriers went, the eight-foot-tall collection of fieldstones held together with crumbling mortar was only slightly more impressive than a wooden stockade fence.

"I wouldn't even need the armor to knock this down," Hans muttered under his breath as he eyed the wall.

Otto smiled in the dark and motioned the wizards to fan out. He gave them ten minutes to get into place then checked the far side of the wall with his magical sight. The nearest guard was fifty feet away and looking in the opposite direction. Clearly Mendelson wasn't expecting trouble. So much the better for them.

An etherial platform lifted him and the others silently over the wall. They landed in the space behind a rundown building and the wall. Another quick look around revealed no interest in them. There was just enough light from scattered torches and what leaked out the windows to allow them to see where they were going.

He flicked his iron ring and bound the nearest guard. The man would be locked in place, unable to move or speak, until Otto released him. Hopefully no one would come to check on him for a while. As soon as someone realized what had happened to him, the game was up.

Hans took the lead as they snuck deeper into the village. For a short, stocky fellow he moved with great stealth. There weren't more than thirty buildings in the town, so reaching the Rolan command post wouldn't take long.

The jingle of an approaching patrol sent them ducking into the shadows between two houses. A moment later six soldiers in brown uniforms marched by. Two of the men were chatting amiably about a serving girl at the tavern and the unit commander said nothing to reprimand them. Clearly the invaders had been having an easy time of it, easy enough that they could go on patrol without a fear in the world.

When they were out of sight, Hans led them out of the alley and toward the village center. The stone building that served as Mendelson's base was directly ahead. A pair of soldiers were on duty out front, leaning on their spears and yawning.

Perfect. Otto bound them in that position. They would pass at least a cursory inspection.

The group hurried over and Hans checked the door. He shook his head. Of course it was locked. His men might be at ease, but Mendelson hadn't struck Otto as a fool. There was no keyhole so it must be barred from the inside.

Fortunately for them, what was a major problem for an ordinary thief, was barely a nuisance for a wizard. Otto sent his sight along with a ten-thread-strong tentacle into the building. No fires burned in either the iron brazier in one corner or the pot-bellied stove in the center of the main room. Everyone must have gone to sleep for the night.

Otto gently lifted the bar out of the brackets holding it. There was a faint clank when the weight fully left them.

He grimaced, but there was no reaction from inside.

"Lord Shenk," Hans said. "A patrol is coming."

Otto set the bar aside and released his spells. The door opened easily and the six of them hurried inside. Hans closed the door and breathed a soft sigh.

So far, so good.

A single door led deeper into the building. The sleeping area had to be there. Otto motioned to it and Hans took up position by the door. The rest of the squad drew their weapons just in case.

When everyone was ready, Otto gathered ether, shaped ten threads through his ring, and nodded.

Hans yanked the door open.

There were five beds beyond the entrance. Startled figures started to sit up.

Otto bound them and released his excess magic. "Someone light the brazier so we can see what we're doing."

Everyone sheathed their blades and Lute got to work with a flint and steel. In short order the glow from the brazier filled the room. The map Otto had seen earlier still covered the table. As he thought, the markings indicated attacks that had already happened. Unfortunately, there was no indication where future attacks might occur.

Perhaps Mendelson could shed some light on the situation.

Otto and Hans went into the sleeping area and searched each bed. Mendelson was the farthest in, his long mustache in disarray and his eyes flashing with hate. Otto hadn't expected a warm welcome.

A quick adjustment of the binding allowed Otto to take control of Mendelson's body. A twitch of his finger brought the man to his feet. He walked like an old man with bad arthritis out to the main room. Luckily for everyone, Mendelson slept in his underclothes.

Otto released his head. "So we meet again. I warned you not to attack Garenland."

"You lot broke the peace, not me," Mendelson snarled.

Otto shrugged. Who did what first didn't matter much at this point. "Where's Villares? What's Rolan's next target?"

"I have no idea on either subject. His Majesty is constantly on the move and I only hear about the raids after the fact. Do you really think they'd tell me anything important living this close to your border?"

Everything Otto could see in the ether indicated Mendelson was telling the truth. It made sense too. When Garenland struck back, Grunewald was the most likely first target. Disappointing as it was, clearly Otto's questions weren't going to be answered here. On the plus side, this was an excellent place to send a message.

"Is there anything you can tell me that would make it worthwhile not to kill you?" Otto asked.

"Even if I could, I wouldn't." Mendelson looked like he wanted to spit in Otto's face. Luckily the magic that controlled his body wouldn't allow him to.

"I suppose there is some honor in that." Otto drew his mithril sword and sliced Mendelson's head off. "Hans, deal with the ones in the back. Everyone else, search for documents. We might find something of interest."

Otto released his spell and Mendelson's body crumpled to the floor.

Half an hour later, a pile of paper that reached to Otto's knee had been gathered. He'd read them later, but for now they had a job to finish.

"Time to wrap this up," Otto said. He went outside and sent up an invisible burst of ether so the wizards would know it was time to attack.

The Grunewald garrison only numbered a few hundred and most of them were asleep when Otto and his team struck. With eleven wizards on their side, the battle was more of a slaughter. Spells and steel cut down enemy fighters as fast as they appeared. When it was over, a single soldier from Rolan knelt in the center of town, bound by magic and without a mark on him.

Otto and Hans stood facing the man. Terror-filled eyes stared back. The soldier's voice trembled as he said, "Please, spare me, my lord. We did no harm to the people of this town."

"You invade my country and claim our territory yet say you did no harm?" Otto asked. "At the very least you and your comrades are thieves. However, enough blood has been spilled tonight. I'm releasing you with a message for your king. Tell Villares that he has until I reach the next Rolan village to surrender. If he hasn't, I'll deal harshly with them. Is that clear?"

"Yes, my lord. But I may not be able to find the king before you reach a village."

"Well, I suggest you look hard. Now leave, before I change my mind."

The soldier scrambled to escape, running as fast as he could toward the main gate. Hopefully he'd locate his master quickly. Otto held no illusions about Villares surrendering, but if he could force a direct confrontation, he was confident in their chances of victory.

"Excuse me?" An old, bald man with a cane came hobbling toward them.

Otto flicked the blood off his sword, sheathed it, and plastered on a smile. "Yes?"

"Not to say that we aren't grateful to be free of the invaders, but what should we do if they return after you leave?"

"Don't worry," Otto said. "I'll arrange a garrison from the Southern Army. We don't want to have to kick Rolan's soldiers out a second time, right?"

"No, thank you, Your Lordship." He hobbled back the way he'd come, seeming content with Otto's promise.

"How long will it take a garrison to arrive?" Hans asked.

"A few days, perhaps a week. In truth, I doubt Villares has the time or people to spare to punish this irrelevant speck of a village. With any luck, he'll be too busy dealing with us."

CHAPTER 2

Uther lay in a puddle of freezing slush and looked down at the entrance to the largest of Straken's mines. He'd been living in the wilds long enough that a little cold no longer bothered him. Below, the Garenlanders had concentrated all the workers and guards at this location. Though he hated to give the bastards any credit, the decision was a smart one. If they'd tried to work all the mines at once, he could have struck the less well defended ones and freed soldiers to add to his meager force.

Not that over four hundred rangers couldn't do plenty of damage—they certainly could—but they couldn't defeat thousands of soldiers backed up by wizards.

He grimaced. Wizards, just thinking about the freaks left a bad taste in his mouth. He couldn't believe Garenland trusted the unnatural creatures for anything, much less trusted them to fight side by side with real soldiers.

Leaving aside his distaste, Uther tried to count. Even though they kept moving around, he was pretty sure there were at least a thousand enemies down there. They'd also been busy. A rough stone wall had been built to control access to the mine entrance. Broken rock and tailings had been piled up to provide cover against archers. While it was far from a proper fortress, combined with their superior numbers the crude defenses gave the Garenlanders a powerful advantage. With his current resources, Uther had no hope of defeating them.

He inched back out of sight then stood. He'd left the rest of the squad he brought a few hundred yards further down the slope where they wouldn't attract attention. Everyone else was back at their new camp. The better weather should make hunting and scrounging supplies easier, but what he really needed was more fighters. The problem was, most of the fighting-age men were in chains and working in the mine.

He shook his head. Maybe the Lady had a brilliant idea. At this point he'd even take suggestions from her.

Uther reached a small glade and the moment he stepped onto the grass, ten rangers seemed to appear out of nowhere. Unlike most of the Straken warriors, the rangers were shorter and less bulky, but fast and agile. They'd switched from winter camouflage to summer. Garenland had decent scouts, he was honest enough to admit that, but none of them could hold a candle to his rangers.

"Majesty, how does the mine look?" asked Dorn, his second-in-command.

"Unassailable, at least for the moment. Much as I hate them, the Garenlanders know their business. Let's get back to camp. I need to think."

The squad formed up around him and they set out. From the glade they followed a narrow path that curved around a steep mountain then descended into a hidden valley about three miles from the mines. It was the sort of place no one was apt to stumble across.

Their tents were set up in a random pattern and disguised by piles of brush, stones, and scraps of cloth. The camp wouldn't fool anyone that looked close, but if you just glanced down into the valley, it might convince someone less familiar with the wilds.

He smiled to himself. What would someone unfamiliar with the wilds be doing out in the wildest part of Straken?

Leaving his men to their own devices, he went straight to his tent. Not having to share was one of the few luxuries he allowed himself.

Uther brushed the flap open and scowled when he found the Lady in Red sitting in his camp chair beside a rough, dirty young man barely in his teens. He took a breath to bawl them out, then caught himself. She knew better than anyone not to bother him unless it was important. If she was waiting for him with this kid, there must be a good reason.

"To what do I owe the honor of your visit?"

"We have a special guest. Olaf here is from Port White. Go ahead and tell Prince Uther what brings you so far from home."

"Yes, miss." The boy's voice cracked and he winced. "Majesty, a ship from Markane has arrived in Port White. Its master says he wants to help us defeat the Garenlanders. Mayor Landen heard you were in the mountains and sent me with a message. The merchant wouldn't deal with anyone but you."

"How did you find me?" Uther asked.

"He didn't," the Lady answered for Olaf. "A patrol of rangers found him, half starved and wandering the trails without a clue where he was. When he told them he had a message for you, they brought him here."

"What do you think of this offer?" Uther hated asking for

her opinion, but he'd had little to do with diplomacy. He'd only visited Markane once and knew next to nothing about the people.

"I think, unless you've found some weakness in the enemy's position, turning down any offer of help would be foolhardy in the extreme. Talking to them costs us nothing and may gain us a great deal."

She was right, damn her. Uther turned his attention back to Olaf. "Did the man from Markane have soldiers with him or anything else you recognized as valuable?"

Olaf shook his head. "Fredrick, that's his name, Majesty, came ashore with six sailors in a small boat. They anchored well out to sea. He could have anything on that ship, though if he brought soldiers, I doubt there could be more than a hundred on board."

Even a hundred soldiers would do Uther little good and from what he knew about Markane, they lacked much in the way of an army. Still, it couldn't hurt to hear what their representative had to say.

"We'll leave tomorrow at sunrise."

⌒

After days of trudging through the wilderness, avoiding roads and towns, and generally sneaking through his own country like a common brigand, Uther and his companions reached Port White.

Straken's sole port wasn't terribly impressive. The docks could only accommodate local fishing ships. Their stone wall was fifteen feet tall and crumbling. The stink of rotting fish lay over everything. One thing it had going for it was a complete lack of Garenland soldiers, for now at least. Uther assumed at some point a small garrison would be assigned to the town.

The townsfolk—women, children, and old men, the same as everywhere else—bowed as he passed. Uther nodded back, trying to keep his expression even regardless of the rage seething in his gut. How his people had been reduced. Much as he loved his father, the king had erred terribly when he tried to destroy Garenland. Not that anyone could have foreseen them turning their wizards into weapons of war.

He shook his head and focused. Mistake or not, what was done couldn't be undone. Now it was up to Uther to make things right so he could hand a restored kingdom back to his father once they freed him from wherever Garenland was holding him.

Waiting for him at the end of the town's main street was a well-dressed man in a blue tunic and white trousers. A gold pin on his breast was the only decoration he wore. Behind him stood six burly, well, burly for outlanders, men in striped shirts and black pants.

"Prince Uther?" The man held out his hand. "Fredrick of Markane. A pleasure to make your acquaintance, Majesty."

Uther's broad, calloused hand engulfed the merchant's small, smooth one. "I welcome you to Straken, though the circumstances could certainly be better."

"Yes indeed. Improving your circumstances is what brings me here. King Eddred and his chief advisor, Lord Valtan, have determined that allowing Garenland to remain in control of the portals and the continent isn't the best idea for anyone."

"And what do your masters propose to do about the situation?" Uther asked.

"While Markane doesn't have many soldiers, we can provide you with magical resources." Fredrick held up a hand before Uther could protest. "I know how you feel about wizards here. The resources I have come in the form of alchemy, specifically explosive vials and ether barrier."

Uther had no idea what either of those things were, though explosives sounded promising. "You're doing this out of the goodness of your heart?"

Fredrick laughed. "Hardly. On credit would be more accurate. You see, Straken is the largest producer of mithril in the world, at least as far as we know. We further know you haven't traded any of your vast store of the metal in years. If we help you retake Straken, payment in mithril would be only fair."

"You have the means to work it?" the Lady asked.

"Not to the extent that Garenland does, but yes, Markane has a number of skilled wizard smiths that can shape mithril. Look at it this way, we're giving you something you can use and asking in return something you can't. A win-win for you, wouldn't you say, Majesty?"

It did seem like a good deal to Uther, which was why he immediately distrusted the offer. "Why don't you show us what we're buying?"

"Excellent idea." Fredrick snapped his fingers and two of the sailors jogged over to a bright white dory tied up to the dock. They came back a moment later, each bearing a coffer twice the size of a loaf of bread. "Here we are."

The merchant opened the first coffer and removed a metal flask. He unscrewed the top and poured a drop of silver liquid on the tip of his finger. "This is ether barrier. When you apply this to your skin, wizards won't be able to target you with spells. The effect only lasts two hours, but for that time you'll be basically magic proof."

He opened the second coffer. Inside were six vials carefully swaddled in mounds of cotton. He took one out and held it up so Uther could see better. There were two liquids inside, one amber and the other blue.

"I think we'd best step outside the wall before I demonstrate this one." Fredrick led the way out the main gate and toward a nearby stand of stubby pine trees. "This is the explosive vial. When you mix the two liquids, they combine to form a volatile compound that explodes upon exposure to air. But perhaps it would be best if you saw for yourself."

Fredrick shook the vial until the liquid turned green then hurled it at the trees twenty yards away. The vial hit the largest trunk dead on and shattered.

The resulting explosion nearly deafened Uther.

When he looked back toward the trees, he found the smaller ones flattened and the big one blown nearly in half. A dozen of those vials would make swift work of the stone defenses Garenland had built around the mine. Shards of flying rock would no doubt whittle their numbers down as well.

"I hope you have more than one case of them," Uther said.

Fredrick smiled. "Many more."

CHAPTER 3

Cypher made his way through the dark streets of Garen. This close to the metal-working district the stink of hot steel and coal smoke mingled to make the air nearly unbreathable. He preferred to avoid the area as much as possible, but for tonight's work, there was no choice. The foundries had let out for the day and the workers were headed home or to their favorite tavern. His target was a particular tavern where wizards were known to gather, the Spark and Flame.

Since receiving the new emperor's permission to establish the Wizards Guild, he and his cohorts had been recruiting throughout the empire, with miserable results he had to admit. Wizards and their skills were rare enough that few of them thought they needed help getting better pay. In fact, the guild's agent in Lux reported that most of the wizards had opened little crystal shops of their own and were doing quite well.

On the one hand, it was good to see his fellow wizards succeeding, but on the other, if they succeeded on their own, convincing them to join the guild became nearly impossible.

He smiled to himself and rounded a corner. It had been easier to convince wizards to join the underground, but now that they had all their rights and freedom, they thought they were home free.

And maybe they were, for now, but he believed sooner or later they would face the same threat they always did, jealous humans that feared their magic. When that day arrived, all wizards would stand together or be killed and enslaved again. Cypher believed with all his heart in what the guild master was trying to build and he'd do anything he could to make it a reality.

Halfway down the street, the Spark and Flame was lit up and the sound of laughter and music emerged from the open door. Sounded like the wizards were having a good time. Maybe if he caught a few of them drunk, he could convince them to join up.

He shook his head as he stepped into the heat and noise of the tavern. How pathetic did that sound?

A few soot-covered faces turned his way, but then quickly returned to their drinks and conversation. On a small, raised stage a bard strumming a lute belted out a bawdy drinking song. Behind the bar, a pretty young woman poured drinks with threads of ether. She handled six with considerable skill, so he suspected seven or eight was her natural limit. That was a lot; Cypher was the third-most-powerful wizard in the guild and he could only wield eleven.

The bartender's cheeks dimpled when she smiled at him. "What can I get you?"

"Wine, please."

She poured without touching either glass or bottle then set the drink in front of him. "Haven't seen you in here before. Are you new in town?"

Cypher shook his head. "I'm with the Wizards Guild. We're looking for new members. With your skill, you could rise high."

"Thanks, but I like it here. Helping Dad with the tavern keeps me plenty busy." A customer ambled up to the bar and she left him alone for a moment. Once she'd served the new arrival she added, "I don't think you'll have much luck. Everyone's pretty happy with the war winding down and all."

"Is your father a wizard as well?" Cypher didn't know why he asked since she clearly had no interest in the guild.

"Nope. Mom and Dad are both regular people. They opened this place and made wizards welcome, so I'd have someone like me to talk to. Before His Majesty and Lord Shenk changed the laws, most taverns wouldn't even let wizards in. We've got more competition now, but most of the regulars remember who treated them right when they didn't have to and stay with us."

At least the wizards knew enough to stick together, even if they didn't do it through the guild. He sipped his wine and looked over the crowd. No one called on their magic, but they all had a faint glow in the ether. The bartender was easily the strongest one here. Not that he expected to find some hidden gem. Most of those with real power had answered the call when Otto began building his war wizards.

Speaking of Otto, one of the universal truths he'd found since starting his recruiting drive was that most of the wizards' first loyalty was to Otto and the emperor. They were the ones that had finally set them free after all.

If the guild were to have any hope of success, he needed to convince Otto to join. How he was going to do that was another matter altogether.

He finished his wine and put the glass on the bar.

"That'll be two silver pieces," the bartender said.

Cypher set the coins beside the glass and a thread of ether swept both away. She really did have talent. Pity she was wasting it here.

He pushed away from the bar and strode into the common room. Even knowing he'd fail, he had to ask if anyone wanted to join.

Lucky for Cypher he didn't take rejection personally.

◯

After a miserable few hours' sleep, Cypher set out for the guild's office in Garen's business district. He had spoken to Otto about a place in Gold Ward, but the young nobleman had pointed out that most of the wizards lived in the business district and would be apt to get turned away if they tried to enter Gold Ward. That combined with the rent of a storefront convinced Cypher to settle for what he had.

He pulled his key out as he approached and unlocked the front door. The staff consisted of three underground wizards and him. He'd worked with them for years helping wizards get settled in Garenland and they were all loyal to the guild.

He stepped inside and stretched his arms over his head. No one else had arrived yet, which suited him fine considering what he had to do.

Just as Cypher had figured, every wizard he spoke to at the tavern the night before had turned him down cold. They were all polite, but firm in their indifference to what he was offering. None of the fools could see the dangers the future might hold. They were all drunk on their newfound freedom.

Maybe they should have waited to establish the guild. It was only a matter of time before something happened between the wizards and normal people. Of course, if they waited, they risked losing what goodwill they'd earned by helping seize control of the portals.

The situation was bleak, but it wasn't his place to decide their next move. That honor, dubious though it might be, belonged to the woman he was about to contact, the guild master. Cypher didn't even know her real name. Neither he nor anyone he'd spoken to called her anything but Guild Master.

The front of the guild office held two tables and half a dozen chairs. If anyone ever showed up, they'd have a place to sit. His office was through a door behind the left-hand desk. He passed through it, ignored his comfortable chair, and called on the ether. The illusion disguising another door vanished and he stepped into the final chamber of the building.

A gesture set a pair of Lux crystals glowing, revealing the chamber in all its modest glory. It measured eight by eight feet. The only notable feature was an inscribed rune circle with a gold-framed mirror in front of it. The mirror was an artifact they'd claimed from a storehouse that used to belong to Lord Karonin. Most of the items inside were beyond their ability to wield, but a few, like the mirror, had come in most handy.

Cypher sat in the circle and sent ether into the mirror. Slowly, the mirror rose off the floor until it was even with his head. Clouds filled its smooth surface before quickly giving way to a cowled, shadowy face.

"Good news I hope, Cypher," the guild master said.

"I'm afraid not. So far my efforts and the efforts of the others have come to little. The wizards see no value in joining us. I've spoken to many and always received the same response: we're free now, what do we have to worry about?"

"And the upstart, Shenk, have you approached him about joining us again?"

"Not yet. He spends little time in Garen and I never know exactly when he might turn up. Speaking to him again is at the top of my list, just as soon as I get the chance."

"Perhaps a few beatings will convince the wizards of the value of our organization. An angry mob of wizard-hating thugs shouldn't be too hard to assemble. See to it and spread the word. If the guild is going to get anywhere, we need to be more aggressive."

A bead of sweat formed on Cypher's forehead, both from the strain of maintaining the connection and the thought of hiring thugs to assault fellow wizards. It went against everything he believed in. But in the end, she was the guild master, not him.

"I'll make the arrangements."

Without another word she severed the connection. Cypher slowly lowered the mirror back into its resting place and stood, his whole body trembling. He blew out a long sigh. He wasn't due to contact the other guild officers until this afternoon. After that he'd need to go looking for leg breakers.

He shook his head. The odds of this ending well didn't merit consideration.

CHAPTER 4

Corina sat easily astride her horse as the army she'd ended up traveling with made its way down the wide trade route deeper into Rolan. Above her palm, a thin, almost indistinct thread of ether wavered. It was getting thicker every time she tried, but she didn't think it was twice as thick yet. Lord Shenk said that it needed to be stronger before she could learn to do something useful.

After joining up with the wizard underground, she'd heard the members talk about the Bliss, but she never dreamed how amazing it would feel. Since learning how to tap into her powers, she'd spent every moment practicing, as much to experience the pleasure it brought as to get stronger.

Not that she didn't want to get stronger. If she was going to help pay back the people responsible for murdering her family, she'd need to get better with her magic. Killing the man that gave the order had been satisfying at the time, but there were so many more that went out of their way to make life miserable for wizards and their families. And all of them had to pay.

Her horse wandered a bit toward the edge of the road and

she guided it back with only pressure from her knees. Like anyone born and raised in Rolan, she could manage a horse without thinking about it.

With a gasp, she released the thread she'd been holding. About fifteen seconds, a new personal best.

"Are you sure you don't want another lesson?" One of the wizards, Antonio, eased his horse up beside her. He made no effort to disguise his lustful gaze as he looked her over. "When we make camp tonight, I'd be happy to show you a few tricks."

"No, thank you. Lord Shenk has offered to teach me himself. If you'll excuse me, I need to talk to him."

She urged her mount further up the line toward the wagon where their leader rode. Of course, he'd made no such offer, but she was happy to lie if it got Antonio to leave her alone.

As she got closer, the outline of the giant armor riding in the bed of the wagon became clear. Corina hadn't seen the massive war machines at work, but she'd heard stories from the wizards that saw them in Straken. The men's voices had trembled when they recounted the slaughter they wreaked.

On the bench, Lord Shenk sat beside his taciturn guard and read one of the ledgers they'd taken from Grunewald. From the scowl twisting his features, whatever he found hadn't pleased him. Finally, he slammed the cover shut and tossed the book in the back.

"Worthless, every bit of intelligence we gathered was worthless. I could have burned it or donated it to the local outhouses for all I learned."

The soldier remained silent, seeming content to focus on the reins and let his master rant.

After a moment Lord Shenk looked her way. "Are you riding beside my wagon for some reason or just on a whim?"

"I thought if I rode beside you, Antonio wouldn't want to

come too close. I told him you were teaching me magic I'm sorry." She blurted out that last bit in one fast, jumbled lump.

He waved off her apology. "I suppose I am teaching you, if not in any formal way. Let's see your thread."

Corina hadn't had much time to rest but didn't dare refuse. She focused hard and soon had the thread formed above her palm. Five seconds later it vanished. This time the Bliss felt more like a thousand bees stabbing her brain.

"You overdid it," he said. "Pushing yourself is fine, but if you feel any pain, that's a sign that you're trying to do too much. Ease back a little, maybe only summon the ether once every hour until you've built up your stamina. On the plus side, I see you're close to having a workable thread. I'd say another week and you'll be ready to try something a bit more interesting."

Corina thrust a fist into the air. That was the best news she'd heard in ages.

"I can see the town in the distance, my lord," the soldier said.

Lord Shenk looked away from her and into the distance. He was doing the thing with his sight again. Corina couldn't wait to learn that one.

At last he said, "They're sending a greeting party. We'll meet them here. Defensive formation, spread the word, Hans."

Hans reined in and leapt down, hurrying along the length of the column.

Lord Shenk turned back to her. "Stay in the rear with Oskar. It looks like we're going to have a battle."

Corina nodded and urged her mount toward the end of the column. It was time to make the dogs of Rolan suffer. She was nearly as eager for that as she was to learn some new magic.

Five thousand spearmen spread out three ranks deep in a square formation protecting their wagons and supplies made an impressive sight. No cavalryman was going to get close without ending up with a foot of steel through his or his horse's guts. That was exactly why Otto had chosen a legion that focused on the spear and shield rather than the usual sword and shield.

The enemy force reined in fifty yards from them. There were only about three hundred Rolan soldiers, hardly a threat given the numbers difference. Still, Otto figured better safe than sorry.

One of the riders, his brown uniform sporting gold horses on the right breast, urged his mount forward. Otto slipped out from the center of the formation to meet him.

"What are your intentions here, Garenlander?" the cavalryman said.

"I should think that was obvious," Otto replied. "I'm looking for Villares. Since the coward refuses to meet us in open combat, I've decided to burn every village I come to until he shows himself."

"That's horrible. War should be between soldiers. Burning the homes of innocent people accomplishes nothing."

Otto shrugged. "Tell that to the people Villares killed in his last raid. I assure you, the innocent people your former king slaughtered did nothing to deserve it. I will kill every man, woman, and child I encounter until Villares either surrenders or brings his army to the battlefield. I'll give the people ahead one chance to flee. They have until we reach the edge of town."

"I can't let you do that."

"Unless you have a few thousand more men hiding somewhere around here... Commander? I'm afraid there's little you can do about it."

"It's captain, not commander. And I can't deny the truth of your observation. But my duty is clear."

"Your duty, Captain," Otto said, "is to protect your people. Dying on our spears won't do that, but if you ride back as fast as you can and warn them of our intentions, you can probably get everyone out before we arrive. Think hard, Captain. If your next move is anything other than retreat, I'll kill you myself."

The captain's face twisted as honor and common sense warred within him. Otto couldn't understand his hesitation. Was it really so much more honorable to die a pointless death than it was to retreat and maybe save a few hundred people? If their positions were reversed, Otto knew exactly what he would have done.

At last the captain wheeled his horse around and thundered back to his men. A shouted order got them turned around and riding back to the town.

So he made the right decision after all. That gave Otto hope that once Villares was dealt with, maybe the people of Rolan would come to accept that life under Garenland's rule wouldn't be so bad. It was a faint hope, but more than he'd gotten when he left Straken.

A good half an hour later, the legion was ready to march again. The journey to the tent village took another half an hour. When they arrived, the last straggler was hurrying out the far end, a pack on her back and a kid at her side. Otto nodded to himself. Better by far if they could draw their true prey out with a minimum of innocent lives lost.

"Wizards!" he shouted. "Launch fireballs!"

Following his own order, Otto launched a volley of six fireballs. Ten more joined them shortly after. That was enough to turn the twenty-odd tents into torches. The whole village went up in minutes.

When it was done, Otto dug the map he'd taken from Grunewald out from the back of Hans's wagon. It was the only thing they'd found worth a damn. From here, the next town was a few hundred miles southwest.

With any luck, Villares would meet them somewhere between here and there. And if he didn't, well, his wizards would be well rested and ready to burn the place down.

CHAPTER 5

Axel paced in front of the mine entrance, paused for a moment to look over the bleak surroundings, then started walking again. There was nothing resembling civilization for hundreds of miles in every direction. Not that the mountains and slowly greening highlands weren't pleasant after a fashion, but they did nothing to alleviate the boredom of protecting the mines.

The several thousand prisoners they'd brought in to dig would occasionally riot. But that wasn't the sort of relief he was looking for. The former soldiers were kept in leg and wrist manacles at all times, so there was little enough they could do. Still, it disrupted production which pleased no one in the capital. Thankfully that, at least, wasn't Axel's problem.

His problem was finding Prince Uther and bringing him, or his head at least, back to Marduke. Axel assumed the best way to do that was to wait here for the prince to make his move. And he was going to make a move, there was simply no way Uther would let his father rot in the mines. Assuming he actually knew they'd brought the former king here.

Axel frowned and went to check on the fortification for the thousandth time. The solid stone structures would provide excellent protection from incoming arrows. The guards were alert and watching every direction. Good, he'd caught one of them napping a week ago and put the man to watching the dig crews. After that, there had been no further issues.

Uther had to know his father was here. They'd made a big show of bringing the former king in, chaining him up, and dragging him into the darkness, but that didn't guarantee word had gotten back to the prince. One of the few things of value Axel had learned from his father, though no one would believe it if they'd met Arnwolf Shenk, was patience.

Father might not have a great deal in most circumstances, but when it came to hunting, he could stay perfectly still and silent while waiting for his prey to appear. And so Axel waited.

"Figured I'd find you out here." Axel turned to find Cobb emerging from the mine entrance. His scruffy second was covered in fine rock dust making his dark beard appear gray. They had a fair barracks just inside the cave mouth, but it was still underground and the air not terribly fresh.

"Cobb. Everything quiet?"

"As a temple after the service. How long are we going to hang around here? We should be out hunting, not hiding in a hole like a bunch of damn moles."

"If you have a suggestion more specific than wandering around the mountains in the hope that we get lucky, I'm all ears. Otherwise, we wait."

Cobb grumbled, but like Axel had no real idea where to even begin looking for Prince Uther. The mountains in northern Straken covered an area the size of half of Garenland. They could literally wander for the rest of their lives and not cover a hundredth of the territory.

"What's that?" Cobb asked.

Axel followed his second's gaze out across the short grass that grew on the hillside above the mine. There was nothing interesting out there. A moment later something flashed in the sun.

That looked like the glint of steel. Axel shaded his eyes for a better look.

When he did, a hundred figures rose up from under camouflage cloaks.

"Alarm!" Axel shouted just as ten of the rangers hurled something down at their position.

The first missile hit short of the low stone wall and exploded like a fireball.

The heat and shockwave forced Axel and Cobb back.

And a good thing too. The next shots were more accurate.

Chunks of stone went flying as the fortifications were blown apart. Reinforcements came boiling out of the mine.

Axel waved his hands. "Get back! Send out the wizards!"

The soldiers pulled up short as more explosions sounded, closer to the entrance. A small group broke off and ran toward those that had fallen.

Axel clenched his jaw but remained silent. If those had been his scouts bleeding out there, he would have gone after them as well.

Finally, a quartet of wizards shouldered their way to the mouth of the cave. Beyond the entrance everything was smoke and dust.

The wizards stared through the haze.

Something moved and one of the wizards raised a hand. Axel grabbed him before he could loose a spell. The group that had gone to rescue the wounded appeared a moment later. Pairs of them carried injured soldiers between them.

"We got everyone still breathing, sir," one of the soldiers said.

"Good. Make a path. Take them to the infirmary." As they passed, Axel grabbed one of the unburdened men. "Did you see the enemy?"

"Couldn't see much of anything."

"Here they come," one of the wizards said.

When they raised their hands this time, Axel did nothing to stop them. No lightning or fire shot out.

"My threads won't connect," a wizard said.

"Mine either," a second added.

Shapes appeared through the haze. Their arms drew back.

"Forget attacking and block whatever they're throwing," Axel said.

The missiles—from closer up they looked like jam jars—came sailing in.

Halfway to the entrance, the jars curved away, exploding to the left and right as the wizards guided them to safety.

The rangers took out more jars and got ready to throw.

This time the wizards were ready.

As soon as the rangers released the jars, they shattered, exploding in the attackers' faces.

The nearest rangers went flying.

Axel held his breath and waited. Slowly the dust and smoke cleared, revealing the ruins of their fortifications and about three hundred rangers. In the center of the group stood a tall, broad figure, small for a man of Straken but still plenty big. He stared at Axel with a cold, hard expression that more than made up for his lack of size.

That had to be Prince Uther.

"Surrender, release our people, and no harm will come to you," Uther said.

Axel would have laughed had the situation been less grim. There was no way Uther would let them live even if they did surrender.

"I won't ask again. Refuse and we'll bring the tunnel down on your heads."

"If you had the power or intention to do that, you would have done it already," Axel said. "I hardly think you're going to kill your own father just to take out a few hundred Garenland soldiers."

"My father's here?" Uther took a step closer then caught himself. "Liar!"

Maybe word really hadn't reached him. Axel glanced at Cobb. "Bring His Royal Highness up here as fast as you can."

Cobb nodded and hurried away.

"I've sent one of my men to get your father," Axel said. "Make another move and you can watch me cut his throat."

The prince stiffened but gave no orders. Axel had bought them a moment's reprieve at least.

He turned to the nearest wizard and whispered, "Can you attack them now that the air is clear?"

"The air isn't the problem." The wizard pitched his voice so no one else would overhear. "Our targeting threads can't reach them. Something disperses them before they make contact."

"You don't actually need to hit them to kill with a fireball, do you?"

The wizard's eyes went wide. "We need to target something, but I suppose the ground at their feet would work just as well. When you give the order, we'll try."

Axel nodded, only marginally encouraged. Relying on wizards that didn't seem to know just what they were doing didn't exactly fill him with confidence. For all that his brother had been a little crazy lately, Axel dearly wished Otto was here right now.

After a tense few minutes, bodies began shifting behind him. Axel looked back in time to see Cobb approaching with a well-chained King Uther in tow. Filthy, bruised, and dressed in rags, the king was a far cry from looking noble.

Axel took him by the arm and drew his dagger. "Here he is. If you want your father to remain breathing, take your rangers and leave."

"Father?" Prince Uther asked.

"What are you doing, boy?" King Uther said. "You know better than to let sentiment control you. If killing these pigs means I die in the process, so be it."

Axel put his dagger to the king's throat. "Shut up. What's it going to be? Does he live or does he die?"

Rage twisted Prince Uther's features. "We'll leave for now, but you will see me again."

The prince and his rangers backed well out of range before breaking into a brisk trot. In a few minutes they were out of sight.

Axel let out a long breath. For now, he was content to let the prince leave and cut their losses.

"Cobb, return the king to his work. Everyone else, let's get busy. I want this position rebuilt and reinforced. When the prince returns, we'll be ready for him."

〜

As Prince Uther led his rangers away from the mine, he couldn't help smiling. His father was alive. Rumors that he'd been taken to the mines had reached him, but until he saw his father with his own eyes, he hadn't truly believed. He clenched his jaw. The Garenlanders would pay for what they'd done to him, especially the one that dared put a blade to his throat.

He would pay the most of all.

On the plus side, the weapons they'd received from Markane's merchant had worked to devastating effect and the ointment had kept the cursed wizards from counterattacking. At least Uther assumed that was what had done it. He knew next to nothing about magic and had no desire to learn.

Now, unfortunately, they were out of both ointment and explosives. Uther had only accepted a small allotment to start since he didn't want to make any promises before he'd tested them. Now that he knew how well they worked, he'd give the merchant whatever mithril he wanted for every bottle Markane could supply.

"Are we returning to camp, my lord?" one of the rangers asked.

"No, Dorn and the rest should have everything packed up and ready to move to the secondary location. One of you take a message to the Lady in Red. Tell her to return to Port White and collect every weapon the merchant has. Dorn and his men can provide protection. She can use her best judgement as to payment. Be sure and cover your tracks. The Garenlanders might be pigs, but they're not stupid. The rest of us are going to look for recruits. There have to be at least some people left willing to fight the invaders."

One of the rangers took off but not directly toward their new camp. Uther put the man out of his mind. All his people knew what they were doing and he trusted them to carry out his orders.

He turned toward the lower slopes. Villages were few and far between in this part of Straken, but they might still pick up a few volunteers.

CHAPTER 6

Sin found herself sitting in the Thirsty Sprite's empty common room two hours before dawn. Only the glow from two lanterns dispelled the gloom. Two of her subordinates were waiting to report while a third droned on about a slowdown at her best Gold Ward whorehouse.

Mentioning Gold Ward did nothing to improve her mood. After Lord Shenk stuck the former king of Tharanault in her villa, the Crow's Nest, she'd been forced to run the guild through Allen's tavern.

While it wasn't a huge deal, having to wait until closing time was a pain. She also felt like she'd lost a little freedom. That, of course, was an illusion. She served at Lord Shenk's pleasure and had ever since he spared her life, an act he could easily undo should she be less than useful. So she didn't complain, at least not to him. Allen might be sick of hearing about her problems, but she owed him nothing.

Unable to stand the droning any longer, Sin waved the fat whoremaster off with the instruction to do whatever he thought best to increase business. She beckoned the next man, Surgan, a six-foot-six bruiser built like a brick wall. He was in charge of her leg breakers and since their business had shifted to serving the Crown, he'd been getting little enough work.

As he sat in front of her, the chair creaking when it took his weight, she made note of the little frown creasing his brow. Usually Surgan was remarkably jolly for a man that made his living hurting people.

"What's wrong?" Sin asked.

"A request came in yesterday, a weird one, figured you'd want to know. This guy reached out to one of my boys looking to get some wizards beaten up."

The breath caught in Sin's throat. "Please tell me you didn't send anyone to attack a wizard."

"'Course not. I did order the stranger followed. Guess where he works?"

Sin shook her head. She couldn't imagine anyone stupid enough to want to hire thugs to attack wizards.

"The Wizards Guild. He went right in that new guildhall they rented."

"That makes no sense," Sin said. "Why would one group of wizards want to assault another?"

"I thought it was strange too, but when you think about it like it was any other guild having trouble recruiting, the move makes sense. Remember when the muleskinners had trouble a few years ago? They hired us to encourage the independents to join up. Didn't take long to convince them either."

Sin looked at Surgan in a new light. Maybe she'd underestimated the big man. A promotion might be in order down the road.

"Whether it makes sense or not, spread the word that none of our people are to mess with any wizards and if the unaffiliated think about taking up the job, deal with them, permanently."

Surgan nodded. "That's what I figured you'd say. Don't worry, I'll make double sure everyone gets the message."

He'd better make sure. Their life expectancy, should Lord Shenk find out one of her thieves attacked a wizard, would be measured in minutes.

Sin tried to focus on the final report, but only got the gist. Her mind was fully occupied by the Wizards Guild matter. Maybe Allen had some way to get in touch with Lord Shenk. Sin wanted to get ahead of the problem and let him know herself.

She considered and immediately dismissed confronting the guild representative that sought out her people. Wizards were totally out of her area. Better to let them sort it out themselves.

❍

When Allen finally dragged himself out of bed, he found Sin up and waiting for him. He'd been seeing a lot of the beautiful guild master, especially since Lord Shenk took over her villa. That was no bad thing, but this morning she looked a little worse for wear. Her hair was matted and dark ridges shadowed her eyes.

As soon as she spotted him, she hurried over. "Do you have some way of contacting Lord Shenk?"

"No, why? Did you get any sleep last night?"

"I couldn't sleep. One of my lieutenants informed me that the Wizards Guild tried to hire thugs to beat up wizards reluctant to join. How do you think he's going to take that?"

Allen didn't need to ask which "he" Sin meant. Their short-tempered employer would certainly not take this news well.

What Lord Shenk would do about the information was another matter altogether. With two groups of wizards involved, the last place Allen wanted to be was in the middle.

"Maybe I can't contact him, but I bet I know someone who can."

"The king?" Sin asked.

Allen laughed. "No, someone that will actually talk to me: the wizard he left in charge of training new recruits. Lord Shenk introduced me to him awhile back in case I needed some magical help when he wasn't around. I don't know if the old man can talk to him over long distances, but even if he can't, he might have some idea what to do about the guild. After breakfast I'll go talk to him. Why don't you try and sleep? You can use my room if you want."

"Thanks, I think I will lie down. If you're still alive, join me later." She sauntered off toward his combination office and bedroom and closed the door.

That was an offer he'd be happy to take her up on, but business before pleasure.

He sniffed. Something was cooking in the kitchen. Allen went through the doors and found Ulf stirring a pan full of potatoes while a thick piece of ham sizzled on the griddle. Even better, a kettle was boiling. Allen badly needed a cup of tea.

An hour later, fed, dressed in his finest outfit, and as ready as he'd ever be to head to Gold Ward, Allen set out by himself. He'd considered bringing Ulf, but he felt better having someone keeping an eye on the tavern. He didn't expect trouble but when you didn't expect it was when trouble tended to show up.

The streets were quiet at midmorning, everyone had already gone to work and wouldn't be out until lunchtime.

Hopefully he could finish his business and be back at the tavern before then.

Outside Franken Manor, the guards asked a few questions, but he'd arrived with Lord Shenk a few times and they all remembered that. No one wanted to get on his bad side by holding up one of his people. Smiling to himself as he walked back across the perfectly manicured grounds Allen was reminded why it was so useful to have a powerful patron.

Silence from the training ground worried him. Maybe Enoch wasn't around. Allen went right to the barracks and found the door shut. He knocked.

The door opened a moment later. Enoch stood there looking just as Allen remembered in his gray robe and white beard. The old man smiled. "Good morning, Allen wasn't it? Please come in."

He stepped aside and Allen entered the building. There wasn't another soul in sight. "Where is everyone?"

"The recruits have all finished their training and been assigned to their new posts. Lord Shenk requested I hang around here in case any new volunteers arrived. Frankly, I don't expect anyone."

"You must be bored."

"A little, but I'm far too old for the battlefield. I'm sure when he returns, Lord Shenk will find something for me to do. But you didn't come all the way across the city to discuss my situation. How may I be of help?"

Allen gave him the short version of what the Wizards Guild was trying.

When he finished, Enoch said, "Have they lost their minds? The guild's purpose is to protect wizards, not bully them."

"My guess is recruitment isn't going well. Can you get word to Lord Shenk?"

43

"No, long-distance communication isn't something I can manage. I can go to Cypher, he's in charge of the guild in Garen, and talk some sense into him. If I can't straighten him out, I shudder to think what Lord Shenk might do when he finds out."

Allen felt exactly the same way. "I can leave this in your hands then? If Lord Shenk checks in with me, I'll have to tell him everything."

"Of course. Hopefully I'll have it sorted out before he returns."

They shook hands and Allen took his leave, content to leave wizard matters to wizards.

CHAPTER 7

Whenever Otto and his troops came within sight of the next tent village, no cavalry came out to threaten them. In fact, he couldn't see any signs of movement. A quick scout via his magical sight confirmed what he thought; the village was devoid of life. Every tent was empty of people and anything of value. That was in some ways a blessing and a curse. A blessing in that he could torch the place without having to kill any innocents, but a curse that there was no one to send word to the former king about what he was doing.

Finally he shrugged and said, "Send a unit to burn the place down. There are no defenders so no reason to waste magic."

The legion commander saluted and barked orders. Soon enough a detachment of spearmen outfitted with torches was quick-marching toward the tents.

"Are you going to burn every town we come to?" Corina had eased her horse up beside the wagon.

"Until I can think of some better way to lure Villares out, yes. Do you have any suggestions?"

"Not me. War isn't my specialty. Anyway, check this out." She held out her hand and conjured a thread. It was thicker than the last one she showed him, almost thick enough to try some basic spells.

"You're getting close," Otto said. "A few more days and I'll teach you a basic self-defense spell."

She brightened. "Promise?"

Otto made a little X over his heart. "Promise."

Corina grinned and rode back to her place in line. In the distance, the tents were already burning and the soldiers were on their way back. Two of them with a third person pinned between them. A messenger perhaps? Otto hadn't seen whoever it was, but one individual wasn't a threat that concerned him and he hadn't looked that closely.

"You seem to enjoy the girl's company, my lord," Hans said.

"She has potential. If it's encouraged properly, she'll make a fine wizard one day."

"An apprentice for you then."

Otto finally turned to look at Hans. "I hadn't really thought of it that way. Certainly there's no formal agreement between us. With all I have to do, I couldn't serve as a proper master anyway. No, I think of myself as more of a short-term mentor."

"Is that how she thinks of you?" Hans asked.

Otto frowned. He didn't know exactly how Corina saw their relationship. He had so much to still learn himself, the idea of teaching someone else seemed absurd. Yet he couldn't deny feeling a certain satisfaction from passing on what he knew. Perhaps when things quieted down, he could make the arrangement more formal.

The soldiers arrived with their prisoner, ending the conversation. The group paused beside Otto's wagon. The lieutenant in charge bowed and said, "We found this one lurking about. He offered no resistance and claims to be a wizard."

Otto narrowed his eyes and looked closer. His white shirt and tan trousers were patched but clean. His lean build suggested he ate well enough. Clearly, he hadn't been mistreated. There was a very faint glow of ether around him. Nothing Otto would have noticed in passing. Whoever he was, he had skill.

"Leave him here, Lieutenant."

"Yes, my lord." The lieutenant saluted and led his men back to their position in line.

When they'd gone, Otto looked down at the new arrival. "And who might you be then?"

"Nicolas, sir. Rumors of your army traveling through Rolan burning villages reached me. I've been hiding for years, but now I thought I could join you and stop pretending I wasn't a wizard."

That would explain how he got so good at hiding his power. "You're not a member of the wizard underground? They're quite good at helping people in your situation."

"No, sir. My father was a wizard and taught me how to hide the gift. Somehow I managed to evade detection."

"Your father?"

"Dead last year. I have no one left so I thought why not take a chance. Better to live free than keep hiding."

Otto hopped down, conjured a powerful barrier of ether and put a hand on Nicolas's shoulder. "You have nothing to fear from us. Did your father teach you how to do anything else?"

"Yes." A dagger appeared in Nicolas's hand out of nowhere and he slammed it into Otto's chest.

The blade scraped across his barrier without penetrating.

Otto sent lightning through his hand into the would-be assassin's body, careful to avoid any vital organs. He wanted the fool incapacitated but alive.

"Lord Shenk!" Hans landed beside him, sword drawn. "Are you hurt?"

"I'm fine." Otto looked down at the crumpled figure and shook his head. "What a stupid cover story. Two generations of wizards going undetected in a society dedicated to finding and enslaving them? What could be more unlikely?"

"He probably figured such a story would garner your pity and get you to lower your defenses." Hans kept the tip of his sword at the assassin's throat. "Shall I end him for you?"

"No, I'm going to have a long talk with Nicolas. And when I'm finished, he'll beg me to kill him. A couple hours after that, I might grant his wish. Let's camp here tonight."

Hans nodded and hurried off to spread the word.

Nicolas groaned and opened his bloodshot eyes. Hopefully that blast of lightning didn't damage his brain. Otto wanted to know who sent him. That way he'd know where to send the remains.

○

Villares sat on his saddle and ate bland stew with the grim determination of a man that knows he needs the nourishment but has no appetite. The smell of his army and the thousands of horses surrounding him didn't affect his hunger. If anything, it was good to be back in the field. It reminded him of the days before his father died and he was forced to assume the throne.

They were all good men, the finest cavalry in the world and

loyal to the death. On the open plains, no enemy should be able to best them. Ten years ago, he would have bet his throne on that. But now the world had changed and not for the better.

Wizards! He nearly spat just thinking about them. What sort of madman let those monsters onto the battlefield? While he hadn't seen directly what they were capable of, Villares had read the reports from his commanders and could well picture the results they described. What the hell good were mortal men against magic?

He set his empty bowl down and a hovering private scooped it up. Even though he was in the field, they still treated him like a king. A king without a castle, or a city, or much of a country for that matter.

One of the boys that served as a messenger approached, then stopped a few feet away as though afraid to say whatever it was he had to say.

Villares scrubbed his hand across his face. "Out with it, boy."

"Yes, Majesty. Our spotters returned and reported that the assassin failed."

The muscle above his eyebrow twitched uncontrollably. He'd hoped that sending a wizard to kill a wizard might work, but it seemed his plan failed. He was only partially disappointed. Such cowardly tactics really were beneath him.

"Is there something else?" Villares asked.

"The Garenlanders burned the village as well."

That was no surprise. He'd ordered all the villages in their line of march evacuated. His people were tough, but most of them had never lived outside of the tent villages. Surviving on the plain as nomads, even temporarily, wouldn't be easy for them. One way or the other, they needed to end this war soon.

"Summon my generals. The time has come to plan our counterattack."

The boy saluted and ran off, all youth and enthusiasm. Villares dearly hoped he didn't get them all killed.

CHAPTER 8

After two days of fretting and debating, Enoch knew he couldn't wait any longer. The news delivered by Otto's spy, Allen, was too worrying to risk further delay. A little after dawn, he set out from the empty barracks for the Wizards Guild's new hall.

He didn't know what Cypher and the guild master were thinking, but threats were certainly not the way to win over anyone's loyalty. And the last thing anyone needed was the guild wizards ending up at war with Otto and those loyal to him.

If he was honest with himself, Enoch doubted the guild would stand much of a chance. With the full power of the empire behind him, Otto was simply too strong. While Enoch didn't know the true state of the guild after all these years, he doubted they could call on more than thirty or so wizards. Otto had over three times that many just in the army. And every one of those men and women were entirely loyal to him and the emperor.

Before he knew it, Enoch stood in front of the guildhall.

The building was nothing special, just a converted storefront. They'd put a sign over the door featuring a book with a wand crossed over it. He shook his head. Anyone that knew anything about magic knew a wand was nothing but an old wives' tale.

There was no movement inside, but hopefully Cypher was around somewhere. He knocked and stepped back to wait.

Happily, the wait didn't last long. Cypher opened the door. His eyes were red and his skin pale and pasty. Clearly running a guild in the open wasn't agreeing with him.

"Enoch, this is a surprise. Finally come to join up?"

"We need to talk. May I come in?"

"Sure, the rest of the members won't be here for an hour or so. Come back to my office, I think there's some brandy in my bottom drawer."

"I'd say you've had enough." Enoch followed him through the empty front room, past a pair of desks, and into a small office.

Cypher dropped into an ill-used chair behind the desk and fished a three-quarters-empty bottle of dark red liquor out of his bottom drawer. "It's been a rough few days. As you may have heard, business has not been booming. I haven't recruited a single new member since we opened and the guild master is getting annoyed."

Enoch waved off the offer of a drink and Cypher took a long pull directly from the bottle. "Is that why you're looking to hire thugs to beat up the people you're supposed to be looking after?"

"You heard about that? I guess I shouldn't be surprised. Have you told your master yet?"

Enoch shook his head. "I was hoping to talk some sense into you before Lord Shenk returns from Rolan. You can't imagine it's going to go well when he finds out."

"Doesn't matter. I can't find anyone to take the job. I'm offering ten times what it's worth and still nothing. What I really need is for your precious Lord Shenk to make a big show of joining then encouraging everyone else to do the same."

"He won't. Otto's only loyalty is to the empire and King—or I suppose now it's Emperor Wolfric."

Cypher snorted and drained the rest of the bottle. "So he said when we last spoke." The bottle shattered against the wall. "They've forgotten! Or maybe they never really understood. Whatever we've gained can be taken away in an instant when the normal humans decide they don't need us anymore. If we don't stand together, all wizards as one, we're vulnerable. Why can't they see that? Why can't he see that?"

"I think Otto sees that very well. He simply has chosen a different path to secure our continued freedom. In his eyes, the empire and its ruler ensure our freedom and by staying in a position where he can influence or even control them, he controls our fate."

"And what do you think?" Cypher asked, his speech suddenly clear. "Is the guild right or is Lord Shenk?"

"I have faith in Otto. How many wizards are there?"

Cypher blinked, clearly taken off guard by the question. "I don't know."

"Take a guess. Personally, I'd say half a thousand in the entire empire. Of those, maybe two hundred and fifty strong enough to really make a difference in battle. Sound fair?"

Cypher nodded.

"Okay, let's say you got them all to join. Do you think five hundred wizards against, what, a million or so ordinary people, would stand a chance? If it ever comes to a fight, we've already lost. Wizards need to show the people that we're on their side. That having us around makes life better and if we were gone, they'd lose a lot. They have to want us to be a part of society."

"They'll never accept us. If you and Lord Shenk believe otherwise, you're dreaming."

"You're not from Garenland, are you, Cypher?"

"No, Tharanault. How did you know?"

Enoch smiled. "I've spoken with a few of the wizards Otto freed from other nations. To a person they remind me of you. Wizards from Garenland have always been more optimistic. The difference between you and them is that they want to grow away from the anger and bitterness. To see their children grow up in a world where they never have to worry about becoming slaves or worse. Otto gives them hope and all you offer is fear. That's why you'll never convince them."

"Nice speech. Maybe I should let you give it to the guild master."

"I'm willing if you think it will help."

Cypher blew out a long sigh. "No, it won't. If anything, she's more determined to build the guild than I am. No words will change that."

"So what happens now?" Enoch asked.

"I have my orders. Will you tell Lord Shenk what I'm doing?"

"I won't have to. Otto has eyes and ears all over the city. He'll know as soon as he gets back. If you're still trying to use violence when he arrives..." Enoch didn't know exactly what Otto would do, but he wouldn't want to be in Cypher's shoes when he returned.

CHAPTER 9

Axel, all his scouts, and five of the most experienced wizards had been tracking Prince Uther and his rangers for a few days and still they'd seen nothing but wilderness. He'd seen enough trees and rocks to last ten lifetimes. There had to be a camp around here somewhere, assuming the prince wasn't just leading them on a merry chase.

At last, an hour before noon, one of the advance parties came jogging back.

"Please tell me you found something," Axel said.

"Yes, sir. What, I'm less sure. Colten says you'll want to have a look yourself."

Axel nodded and the main group double-timed it to where the advance party waited. Colten and his men stood around a patch of dirt that to Axel looked exactly like all the other patches of dirt around here.

"Report."

"They stopped here," Colten said. "The bulk of them turned south while one or two kept going west. Someone did a fair job of wiping out the tracks, but you can still just make out where their boots left impressions."

Axel couldn't see any such thing, but he trusted the young scout. "Cobb, where's that map?"

"Here, my lord." Cobb fished a many-times-folded map out of his pack and handed it to Axel.

After a moment of study Axel pointed to an area of the mountains. "We're about here. The mountains turn to forest about another day to the west. South is Straken proper, where what's left of the population lives. My guess is the main group is Uther and he's hoping for reinforcements. He won't find much, but he might pick up a few. The question is, where are the other two going?"

"Maybe their new camp is in the forest," Cobb said.

Beyond the forest was a circle marking a town labeled Port White. Axel seriously doubted anyone in Straken had the know-how to fashion those exploding jars. However, there might be someone in Markane that did. Port White would be the perfect place to meet with someone from the island kingdom. At the very least they needed to check it out.

"Fourth and fifth squad, return to Marduke and warn General Varchi that the prince is headed south and may be planning to stir up trouble. The rest of us are heading west. I want to know what those two are about. You can follow them, Colten?"

"As long as we don't get into rocky ground, yes."

"Then let's go."

For two days they followed a path visible only to Colten. Axel knew next to nothing about magic, but he suspected there had to be a little of it in the scout's uncanny tracking skills. On the afternoon of the third day, as the group approached the crest of a ridge, Colten waved them down.

Everyone crouched and Axel worked his way to the front of the group. "What is it?"

Colten pointed at the ground by his feet. There was a jumble of tracks so thick even an untrained soldier would have seen them. "Our guys met some of their friends here and they continued on over the ridge. We must be getting close to their camp and I didn't want to barge into anything."

"Good thinking."

Using hand signals, Axel dispatched Cobb to the left and another group to the right. The advance groups would check things out just to be sure.

Ten minutes later a piercing whistle filled the air. That was the all-clear signal. Axel stood and looked over the ridge. Cobb and the others were gathered in a clearing that had clearly once been a camp. There were fire pits, well-worn paths, and signs that tents had once dotted the area.

It was a short walk down to the clearing. When Axel arrived Cobb said, "We missed them by a couple days I'd say. They cleaned up after themselves anyway. Other than a few scuffed-up patches of dirt and ash piles, you'd never know they were here."

"I wouldn't say that." Colten straightened, a green glass bottle in his hand.

Axel took it and sniffed the mouth. Wine for sure. He studied the bottle, checking for anything that might tell where it came from. He found it at last on the bottom, a seal depicting a leaping dolphin.

"This came from Markane," Axel said. "I was right, they are getting help from the island."

"How do you know?" Cobb asked.

Axel tossed the bottle aside. "A year before I left, Father received a case of wine with the same maker's mark on the bottom from a merchant looking for a deal on apple brandy. He didn't get it, but Father remarked on the quality of the vintage. That was the only reason I looked closely at the bottle. It seems Prince Uther is getting more than magic from them."

"We don't need to follow the tracks now. We'll make straight for Port White. Hopefully we can grab them before they pick up any more explosives."

"We may just do that," Colten said. "They've got a wagon with them now. That will force them to avoid rough terrain while we cut straight through the forest."

Axel bared his teeth in a fierce grin. Finally, things were going his way.

♀

Despite Axel's best efforts, he and his men arrived behind Uther's group. Not by much, but that didn't matter. The town of Port White wasn't huge, but it had a wall and guards. That was more than enough to keep out Axel and his small force. They'd settled for taking up position on a knoll overlooking the town. It allowed an unobstructed view of Port White and the ocean beyond.

Two things interested Axel. The first was the massive trade ship anchored offshore. It flew no flags, but it didn't take a genius to figure out it must have come from Markane. No other nation, not even Lux, had vessels that big. The second thing that drew his eye was a figure in bright red mingled among the darker forms of the rangers. It seemed Uther had sent the Lady in Red to handle his negotiations.

Axel grinned. He'd long wanted to wipe the smile off her arrogant face. Looked like he was about to get his chance.

After the forced march his scouts were huffing and puffing.

It was bound to take a while for the rebels and Markane's representative to finish up their discussions. This would be an excellent chance to get some rest.

"We'll keep watch in shifts," Axel said. "One squad per shift. First squad and I will take the first two-hour shift. Everyone else get some sleep."

As the others stretched out wherever they could find a spot free of rocks or brush, Axel silently cursed Otto's absence. If ever there was a time he could have used his brother's talent for long-distance spying, this was it. He doubted any of the wizards he had with him could pull the trick off. If they could, one of them certainly would have spoken up.

Better safe than sorry. "Can anyone among the wizards use sight-extending spells like my brother?"

He was met with a chorus of head shakes. Axel swallowed a sigh, not surprised but still disappointed.

Soon enough he was surrounded by soft snores. His watch passed without anything happening and after two hours, Axel settled himself down to sleep.

At first light the next day, Axel once again found himself on watch. Tiny shapes were moving around near the wagon, shifting boxes and loading crates. Looked like they'd be moving soon. Time to wake up the guys and get into position.

An hour later, they were hiding in the evergreens that lined the road out of Port White. Axel had chosen to set up on the southern branch of the road on the assumption that the targets would be going to meet Prince Uther. If he was wrong, they were going to have a hell of a time getting ahead of the wagon on the eastern branch.

Axel said a silent prayer to any angel or demon that might be listening. He needed this ambush to work. If a wagonload of those explosive jars fell into Uther's hands, he could kill thousands of Garenland soldiers. Far too many citizens had fallen to Straken fighters under Axel's watch. Damned if he was going to let any more die.

One of the scouts further up the road waved. The wagon was on its way.

Axel let out a long sigh. The first part of his gamble had paid off, now he needed to follow through and close the deal. They also needed to be damned careful not to set off the explosives in the wagon. While he didn't especially care if the Lady and her guards died, he doubted they would be the only ones caught in the blast.

"Archers ready, pass the word," Axel said. With the polished flat of his dagger, he caught the sun and flashed a signal to Cobb on the opposite side of the road.

Up and down the line, arrows were fitted to strings. Axel eased his sword partway out of its sheath to loosen it, then slid it back. He didn't want a glint of metal to give them away.

A few minutes later, the wagon appeared. The Lady and a burly ranger sat on the bench, while the rest of the group marched along on either side. Axel counted forty altogether. A strong force, but badly outnumbered by his scouts. With a little luck, this should end quickly.

When the wagon was in position, Axel pointed.

The archers stood and loosed a volley into the guards. Rangers dropped and the survivors scrambled to get to the other side of the wagon.

The moment they did, Cobb's team loosed, felling even more of them.

Axel and the swordsmen leapt into the road. "Surrender!"

The wagon driver reached around for one of the crates. He made it halfway before freezing in his tracks. One of the wizards had bound him, just as they were instructed.

The Lady in Red glared at Axel but remained silent. The tension grew as those rangers still free to move looked at each other, clearly trying to decide if a quick death in battle would be better than prison and the mines.

It didn't take them long to decide.

With a roar, the rangers drew their curved blades and charged.

They managed a few steps before the archers cut them down. If they had been anything but rangers, Axel might have felt bad. As it was he'd had enough brawls with the bastards to be happy not to have to worry about guarding them had they surrendered.

That left him with two prisoners, the Lady and her driver. One of them was bound by magic and the other remained as still as if she was as well.

"Where's Uther?" Axel asked as he sheathed his sword.

She remained silent.

"You're going to have to talk eventually, might as well do it now and save yourself some discomfort."

"I'll never talk. Do your worst, you can't break me." She sounded so certain.

Axel shook his head. "Maybe I can't, but if you won't talk to me, you'll talk to my brother when he arrives. I promise, what Otto will do to you won't be pretty."

"Otto Shenk, Wolfric's pet wizard? He's your brother?"

Axel nodded. "He's grown a lot more disagreeable over the last year. I think all the pressure of building an empire is getting to him. No doubt taking out his frustrations on you will do him good."

"What are we going to do with this junk?" Cobb jerked a thumb toward the wagon.

Axel wasn't going to take any chances with such dangerous

material. He glanced at the still-paralyzed ranger. Did he really need two prisoners? He doubted whoever the ranger was knew more than the Lady.

"Someone tie her up and cut that guy's throat."

He went to the rear of the wagon and opened the first crate. There were a dozen glass jars filled with two types of liquid. Those were the explosives. A second crate of a different style yielded metal flasks. Axel took two of the explosive jars and one of the flasks. No doubt Otto would want to study them.

"Load the bodies in the wagon, carefully," Axel said.

Half an hour later, the wagon was piled high with dead rangers. The scouts moved a safe distance away and Axel threw one of his two jars at the wagon. It shattered but didn't explode as he expected. After a second's delay, the wagon burst into flame.

"Run," Axel said.

They did and a good thing too. When the wagon exploded, a pillar of flame shot fifty feet into the sky and the noise nearly deafened him.

"Let's get back to Marduke," Axel said. "The sooner this witch is in a cell, the happier I'll be."

CHAPTER 10

Otto watched with just the hint of a smile as Corina finally conjured a thread strong enough to do something useful. They were riding together in the bed of the wagon while Hans drove. When it became clear a few days ago that she was close to making a breakthrough, he began debating which spell to teach her first. Binding would be simplest, but he didn't have an iron ring for her. Lightning would be the next most useful.

"How was that?" Corina asked when she finally let the thread vanish.

"Good. You're ready to learn your first spell."

Her smile nearly split her face. "Which one?"

"I think lightning would be a good one to start. It won't be terribly strong, but if you get into trouble, you'll certainly be able to make someone think twice. If you can strike their head or heart, you might even kill them. Sound interesting?"

"Everything about magic is interesting. What do I do?"

"Let's see if you can get a spark. Conjure a short thread, not more than an inch long, and slide it into your index finger. Just beyond the tip."

She did as he said with only the slightest hesitation as the ether pierced her flesh. It was painless but disconcerting. Otto's whole body shivered the first time he did it.

"Good. Do you feel the energy there? Like a tingle."

Her forehead crinkled. "There's something, but it's really weak.

"That's what you want. Will the energy to merge with the thread and follow it out of your finger."

"I'm not sure what to picture," she said.

Otto frowned as he considered how best to explain. At last he said, "Try to think of the thread like a tube and the energy as water flowing through it."

"Okay." She glared at her finger so hard he half expected her hand to burst into flame. "Nothing's happening."

"Relax. Don't try and force it, just let the ether flow."

Corina made a visible effort to relax. The moment she did, a spark leapt from her finger.

"I did it!"

"Yes, very good. Now—"

Before he could continue his instruction, the girl wrapped her arms around his neck and hugged him. Otto gave her an awkward pat on the back. From the front of the wagon he would have sworn he heard Hans chuckle. He let it pass without comment. There was little enough for amusement out here.

After a moment Corina got herself under control and let go. "Sorry. That was my first real magic and I got excited. What were you going to say?"

"I was going to say that now you need to practice creating the spark as quickly as you can. Under a second would be ideal, but I don't expect that right away. And don't forget to keep practicing your threads. Now that you can make one, try and make a second."

She stared at him. Maybe that was too much too soon. "I can only hold one for about half a minute. Two would probably kill me."

"It won't kill you, but it will wear you out quickly. Practice—"

"Lord Shenk," Hans cut into their conversation.

Otto was getting thoroughly sick of being interrupted midthought. "What?"

"There's something coming. A huge cloud of dust is on the horizon."

He stood and sure enough a brown cloud hung over the plains. Quick as thought Otto sent his sight soaring out. What he found did little to improve his mood.

He blinked and said, "Villares is driving a massive herd of cattle toward us. His cavalry is following in its wake."

"They mean to trample us," Hans said.

"And break our formation. Stop the wagons, power up your armor and form a wedge in front of the army. Corina, find Oskar and stay with him."

Otto leapt out of the wagon as soon as they stopped. While Hans organized his squad, Otto went to the legion commander and explained the situation. When he finished the commander said, "My men are strong, but they can't stand against a charge of cattle."

"I'm aware. Don't worry. Get everyone in position behind Hans and the armor and be ready to engage the enemy cavalry. My wizards and I will make certain to turn the cattle."

The commander saluted and set about getting his people into position. Otto's next stop was the group of wizards he brought. They all looked a bit nervous as he approached. Combat on the open plains was quite a bit different than fighting a siege. On the plus side, the enemy only had cattle, not other magicians.

"We need to make a wall of fire," Otto said. "That will turn the cattle and protect the legion."

"Master Enoch didn't teach us how to make a fire wall," one of the Garenland wizards said.

"Don't worry, I'll handle the spell, you just fuse your ether to mine and extend it. Hurry, there isn't much time."

Indeed, as they rushed to their places in the center of the formation, the ground was already shaking from the approaching herd. Hans's squad in their magical armor knelt in a wedge in front of the spearmen, swords drawn and driven into the earth for extra balance.

"How long, Hans?" Otto shouted.

"Fifteen seconds."

Otto grimaced. He wasn't going to get more than one shot at this.

He drew his mithril sword and sent thirty threads through it before forming them into two thick tubes, one on either side of the legion. Finally, he rubbed his fingers to generate heat and sent it through.

Ten-foot-high walls of fire sprang up. They ran half the length of the gathered men.

The roar of the cattle was like thunder. Otto coughed as the dust rose but didn't lose focus.

One by one the other wizards extended the wall until it ran the full length of the battle line.

And not a moment too soon. The herd broke around the massive armor, saw the flames, and shied away. Otto could barely see them through the blaze.

Sweat broke out on his forehead and not from the heat. Maintaining the flames took everything he had.

"Clear!" Hans shouted.

Otto and the other wizards immediately released their spells.

The armored men stood and wrenched their swords free of the earth. A horrid crash of steel on steel was mingled with the screams of men and horses.

The spearmen shifted left and right, forming a phalanx and stabbing into the enemy horsemen.

Otto knew he needed to lend a hand, but right now it took all he had just to stand. A few of the others hurled weak spells into the enemy formation, but they hardly made a dent. This fight at least was going to be settled by muscle instead of magic.

The fight dragged on for nearly fifteen minutes before the noise died to nothing. Otto's breathing and heart rate were back to normal as he stepped around the wall of spearmen. Hundreds of men and horses lay dying on the ground, thankfully most were wearing Rolan uniforms.

Most but not all. The soldiers trained in first aid hastened to help their comrades, binding wounds and preparing to carry them back to the healers in the supply train a few hours behind them.

Hans climbed down from his armor seeming none the worse for the fight. "I swear, my lord, kneeling there with a few hundred cattle rushing at me is the strangest and most terrifying thing I've ever faced on the battlefield."

"Let's hope it stays that way. Gather your men and let's see if we can find Villares."

A few minutes later they were knee deep in bodies. It was easy to tell which ones were killed by the armor, since they were all in multiple pieces. Hans kicked over a corpse but found only an ordinary soldier.

"You didn't see him during the fight?" Otto asked.

Hans shook his head. "I only focused on uniforms. Slice brown and avoid black and gold. The fight moved too fast for anything else."

Otto nodded, disappointed but not surprised.

A pained shout drew him to the left. Two wounded Rolan soldiers were attempting to shift a dead horse off a pinned third man. They noticed Otto and the others coming and drew their sabers.

"Hans, my magic is still a little under the weather. Would you mind?"

"Certainly, my lord." Hans drew his own sword and the others followed suit.

The fight ended as quickly as it started. Hans and his men weren't considered the best for no reason. They sheathed their blades and Hans looked down at the trapped man. "I found him, Lord Shenk."

Otto let out a sigh of relief and hurried over. Sure enough, Villares had his right leg trapped under the dead horse. He appeared unharmed otherwise. Whether that was good luck or not, Otto wasn't sure.

"Spare me your gloating and finish it," Villares said.

"You're hardly in a position to make demands. Someone fetch Corina up here please."

Hans gave a nod and one of the guys ran off.

"Who's Corina?" Villares asked.

"One of your victims, an innocent girl with the good fortune to be born a wizard. Her parents were murdered because they refused to let her become a slave. She survived and I've been giving her pointers. She's a good kid who didn't deserve to lose her parents because of an accident of birth."

Villares snarled and clutched his leg. "Wizards aren't really human. You and all like you are something else. Demons, monsters, I don't know, but not human. We keep them under control so the rest of the people can go about their day without fear of having their minds twisted or getting burned to a crisp because they bumped into the wrong person in the market."

Otto shook his head. "Yes, far better if they get robbed and stabbed by a proper human. As if they won't be just as dead."

There was clearly no point in continuing the conversation. Villares was as set in his ignorant beliefs as the rest of the fools that tried to destroy Garenland.

"Lord Shenk?" Corina approached with the soldier Hans had sent.

She looked a little pale. This was probably the first time she'd ever set foot on a real battlefield. It wasn't a nice place and if Otto had his way, none of the wizards would ever have to see another one. If that wasn't wishful thinking, he didn't know what was.

"Come here, Corina, there's someone I'd like you to meet." She joined him and stared down at the fallen king. "This is Villares, your former ruler. He made the laws your parents broke to protect you. You could say he is the author of your troubles. Would you like to kill him?"

Corina looked at him with wide eyes. "Kill the king? Me?"

"Former king, technically. Oskar said you already killed the man that ordered your parents' deaths. Well, this is the man that commanded him. I give him to you as a reward for your hard work. You can try your lightning spell. I'll walk you through it."

She looked from Villares to Otto. "When I stabbed the

cavalry commander it was in the heat of the moment. I didn't even think about what I was doing. But this... it feels like murder."

"It's no more murder than what the hangman does. He's going to die, the only question is who ends his worthless life."

Corina shook her head. "I don't think I can."

Villares coughed and laughed at the same time. "Stop pretending you care about human life. Miserable wizard. If I was free, I'd cut your throat myself."

Corina's expression hardened. "What do I do?"

Otto smiled. "Conjure a thread and send it into his chest and through his heart. No need to rush, make sure you find the right spot. Now in a real battle you couldn't take your time like this, but for now it's fine."

He watched her guide the wisp of ether into Villares, fumble around, and finally slide it through his heart. The magic was so fine Villares's natural defenses didn't even register it as a threat.

"Good. Now connect the thread to the spark in your finger like we practiced earlier."

Corina did as he said and a moment later a weak bolt of lightning streaked out and into Villares who howled and thrashed.

She started to pull back but Otto said, "Don't stop until he's dead. You'll feel it when the life is burned out of him."

Corina kept the lightning going for another five seconds. When she ended it, a black circle had been burned in Villares's still chest. Otto gave her shoulder a squeeze as she gasped for breath. "Well done. Like anything else, killing with magic gets easier the more you do it."

"I think I need to rest." Corina ran back toward the wagons.

"Little hard on the girl, weren't you, my lord?" Hans asked.

"She's only two years younger than me. Despite our best efforts, there are still plenty of people like Villares out there. People who would kill a wizard without a second thought just because of what we are. Every wizard, her included, needs to know how and more importantly have the will to strike down anyone that threatens them. This is the hardest part of being a wizard, Hans. When you kill with magic, you feel it down to your soul. If they can't accept that, no wizard will be safe."

Hans nodded. "What now?"

"Now you all head back to Rolan City. I need to tell Wolfric that Villares and his resistance has been crushed."

With his strength now sufficiently recovered, Otto became one with the ether and vanished.

CHAPTER 11

Rested, fed, and having made his report to Wolfric, Otto found himself once again traveling through the portal to Straken. At least this time he didn't have to commandeer anything from General Varchi. He had no trouble doing that when he had to, but the good general's attitude got on his nerves and if he got on them too much Otto feared losing his temper. Replacing a general wasn't a task he needed right now.

The lights of the ether faded as he stepped out into the nearly complete fort. All the towers were in place and connected by walls. The final touches were being put on the gatehouses that would control access to the portal. Not that Otto expected a great deal of trade between Straken and the other provinces, but he had no intention of taking chances.

The soldiers all knew him and knew enough not to pester him with questions. Korgin should be around here somewhere. The infiltrator had been reassigned to serve as a general overseer who reported to Otto rather than General Varchi.

"Lord Shenk!" Speak of the devil.

Korgin came trotting over from one of the barracks that had been built to house the portal guard. He wore a proper uniform of black and gold today. Which made sense given that all the locals had been sent on their way. Only Garenland soldiers remained in Marduke.

"Korgin. I trust all is well?"

"In some respects yes and in others no. Marduke is peaceful and nearly back together. We had no trouble evicting the residents. In fact, most were eager to leave. They really do hate us."

That was one fact Otto didn't need reported to him. "The problems?"

"Yes, Prince Uther attacked the mines. There was some loss of life, but none of the prisoners were freed. Your brother has more details. He requested you speak to him at Castle Marduke when you arrived."

Otto frowned. Axel should be guarding the mines, not wasting his time here. Whatever he wanted must have been important. "I'll head there directly. No trouble with the general?"

"None. He seems to enjoy playing governor, holding court with his junior officers, even having a feast now and then. Nothing excessive," Korgin hastened to add when he saw Otto's reaction. "He leaves most of the day-to-day business to the unit commanders and they seem happy enough not to have him looking over their shoulders."

"Alright. Well done, Korgin. Once we have matters here fully under control, I'll see about getting you some downtime in the capital along with a nice bonus for your excellent work."

Korgin bowed. "I'm honored by your praise, Lord Shenk."

Otto nodded and turned toward the exit.

The walk to Castle Marduke took around ten minutes. The guards manning the gates recognized him at once and hastened to move out of the way. Otto paused and chose one at random. "Where is Axel?"

"I believe Commander Shenk and his scouts have moved into the old guard barracks, my lord." The nervous soldier pointed at a low, single-story structure built along the eastern wall.

"Thank you."

Otto marched directly to the barracks door and knocked. The door opened a moment later and Axel's surly second-in-command appeared in the gap. His eyes widened just a fraction when he found Otto waiting.

"Lord Shenk. He said you'd be by eventually."

"Where is my brother?"

"In the dungeon questioning our prisoner, not that he's having much luck. The bitch is tougher than I would have believed. We've tried everything and she hasn't said a word. Your brother believed only magic would loosen her tongue."

"Loosen whose tongue?"

"I assumed you knew. We captured the Lady in Red about a week ago. She's been in the dungeon for the last two days and has so far resisted every trick we tried. Didn't dare go too hard. She can't answer if she's dead after all."

Otto took a moment to process the news. "How did you manage that?"

"Long story. Probably better if I let the commander tell you himself. Follow me." Cobb turned and shouted to one of his men that he'd be back shortly.

They entered through a side door and followed a curving hall to a set of stairs that led to the basement. Otto vaguely remembered the passage from his brief scouting run when they first arrived but was glad to have someone show him the way.

As they started down the steps Otto asked, "There was no structural damage from the collapsing tunnel?"

"No, none. Whoever dug that trap knew what they were doing. Other than cleaning up some broken rock that slid into a storage room, everything was fine."

They stopped outside a heavy, iron-banded door. A muffled scream came from deeper in.

"Sounds like he's still at it. You can go on in." Cobb held the door then closed it behind Otto.

A short walk past half a dozen empty cells brought Otto to the torture chamber. It was every bit as well equipped as Father's. The only light came from a glowing brazier. Axel stood over a prisoner bound to the rack.

He turned as Otto approached. "I didn't really expect you so soon. Things must have settled down in Rolan."

"Villares died yesterday and his army is broken. There'll be some cleanup work, but nothing that requires my full attention. I see you've caught quite a prize."

"She might be a prize, but I can't crack her open. Want to take a shot?"

Otto stood beside his brother and looked down at the Lady. All the haughty confidence was gone now. Her famous red dress was little more than rags and burn marks marred her smooth skin. She made a pitiful sight, not that he felt any pity for her.

"Time flies, doesn't it?" Otto said. "I don't imagine you thought the next time we met would be under these circumstances."

She glared in sullen silence.

"No advice to offer me today? Shame. I suppose we should get started."

Otto flicked his iron ring and bound her with her eyes

open. The magic he was going to try wouldn't work if she couldn't see. Drawing on the ether, he conjured a spinning, multicolored wheel. As she stared at it, he sent threads into her brain, activating the section that controlled relaxation and pleasure.

Pain was a fine thing, but it had many limits. Pleasure, on the other hand, was so much more versatile. Moment by moment the tension left her and after ten minutes she was calm and fully relaxed.

"Uther's in trouble." Otto spoke softly, gently, like a lover whispering in her ear. "We have to find him. Only you can save him."

"Split Rock. I have to meet him with the weapons at Split Rock." She spoke like someone in a dream.

"Of course, Split Rock. I'll send a warning at once. His plans will need to be changed as well. What were they again?"

"Find more fighters then free his father and the other prisoners."

Otto smiled and nodded. "Thank you. That was wonderfully helpful. You should go to sleep now. Poor thing, you look exhausted."

A thread of ether slipped into the part of her brain that controlled sleep and soon she was out.

Otto nodded toward the door. Once they were outside the dungeon he asked, "Did that mean anything to you?"

"I've never heard of Split Rock, but this is one of the weapons she was talking about." Axel took a jar filled with some strange liquid out of his satchel. Two liquids of different colors filled it nearly to the top. "These things explode on impact like a fireball. They had a whole wagonload of them. I destroyed it save for this sample."

"A prudent decision." Otto took the weapon and looked it over. The jar had to be alchemy of some sort.

"That's not all." Axel held a metal flask in his hand. "This stuff kept our wizards from targeting them with spells."

Dangerous as the explosives were, the greater danger by far was something that could render magic ineffective. He'd have to take both items back to Garen and see if Ulf knew what they were.

"Where did Uther get something like this?" Otto asked.

"Markane. I saw one of their big trading ships anchored off the coast."

Otto snarled. So Valtan had finally decided to join the fight. Fine. He would have preferred to avoid conflict with the island nation, but if they were going to provide his enemies with something like this, Otto had no choice but to act.

"I'll look into this myself. Is there anything else?"

"The prisoners riot about once a week. It's more of a nuisance than anything, but if we keep having to kill a bunch of them every time, soon we'll have no workers."

"Great. Maybe I can do something about that as well. The Lady can stay in your care, at least until Wolfric decides what he wants to do with her. Well done, Axel. I'll return as soon as I can figure out what to do about your unruly prisoners."

Otto hurried back toward the portal. He wanted to return as quickly as possible and find out what he was up against. He also needed to figure out how to convince Markane to stay out of his business.

CHAPTER 12

Otto took the portal back to Garen rather than
traveling directly through the ether, both to
conserve his own strength and to drain Valtan's. If
the Arcane Lord wanted to go to war, Otto would do everything he could to hurt him. To someone as powerful as Valtan,
it was surely at most a minor annoyance, but for now it was
the best he could manage.

The guards watching the Garenland side of the portal
saluted when he emerged and opened the fort's gate. Otto
strode straight through before turning toward the Thirsty
Sprite. It was approaching noon so hopefully Allen and Ulf
were awake and alert. Not that it would bother Otto to zap
them out of bed, but he'd found he got better results when he
avoided that sort of thing.

Twenty yards from the tavern, he slowed. Two big, burly
men were on guard outside the door. That was new. Had
something happened or was Allen just taking extra precautions? Otto dismissed the question at once. He trusted Allen to
know what was best for his business.

The moment Otto got close, the two guards moved to block him. "Tavern's closed," the right-hand man said. "Come back this evening."

Otto smiled. His annoyance with matters in Straken had left him in a foul mood. Lucky for him it seemed two idiots were volunteering to cheer him up.

"You don't recognize me, do you?" Otto asked. Surprising as it was, apparently at least a few people weren't familiar with his face yet.

"I don't care if the emperor himself sent you. Sin isn't seeing anyone until the tavern opens. So get lost." The thug reached out to shove Otto.

Otto enhanced his body with twenty threads of ether, grabbed the approaching wrist, and squeezed. Bone snapped and his hand twisted around, so his fingers were pointing back at his chest.

The thug howled in pain. Otto released him and the man fell to the ground clutching his arm.

Otto turned to the second man. "Is the tavern still closed?"

The thug looked from Otto to his partner and back again. That the door wasn't already open was an insult. Maybe he'd break both of this one's arms.

Lucky for the guard, the door opened and Sin's lovely face appeared in the gap. She took one look at Otto before hastening to open up the rest of the way. "Lord Shenk. We weren't expecting you. Please, forgive my men's rudeness. Come in. Allen's just getting ready for breakfast. We'd be delighted if you'd join us."

"Thank you. And don't worry, I've already given your guards a lesson in manners." Otto glared at the still-standing man. "They won't be getting a second."

Otto stepped inside and she closed the door behind him.

The tavern appeared exactly as he remembered. A single table had the chairs down, four of them, how convenient. From the kitchen came the sounds of someone working.

Sin ran a hand across his shoulders. "You're tense. Sit, relax. Can I pour you a drink?"

"This isn't a social call. What's with the guards anyway? Are you having problems?"

"No, no problems. Since I've been running the guild from here, I get visitors at all hours. When I need a break, I find putting guards on the door keeps all but my most important lieutenants away. I neglected to tell them my orders didn't apply to you."

"I believe they understand that now. How fare your house guests?"

"The former king and his daughter have had a few visitors, mostly merchants eager for advice on what to sell in Tharanault for the best profit. Nothing of real import has been discussed. The pair venture out only rarely and my people keep a close watch. If they're plotting anything, they're doing it in their minds."

Otto nodded. That was exactly what he wanted to hear. Hopefully Liatos and his daughter would accept their new situation and live quiet lives.

"How long were you planning to keep them at the Crow's Nest?" Sin asked.

"For the rest of their lives. If you need a new base, I can arrange to fund the purchase. Keeping the royals somewhere secure and under guard is important. Many of the people in Tharanault remain loyal to them which makes them useful. But your work is valuable as well so let me know what you need."

Sin's smile would have curled the toes of a less bitter man.

"What was all that shouting?" Allen emerged from his office, took one look at Otto, and added, "Never mind. Lord Shenk, this is a surprise. Have you brought matters in Rolan to a close?"

"More or less. My problems now are in Straken. I need the opinion of an alchemist."

"Ulf's fixing breakfast. He should be out shortly. While we wait, did Sin tell you about the Wizards Guild?"

Otto turned to the beautiful thief. "What about them?"

"I was just getting to that when you came out, Allen. The local guild rep was looking to hire some of my leg breakers to rough up any wizards that didn't want to join." Sin hastened to add, "We refused of course."

"I warned them not to try and force anyone to join." Otto clenched his fist. "It seems I'll need to be more emphatic."

The kitchen door opened and Ulf emerged with a laden tray of food. It served to break the tension and Otto finally sat down. He wasn't especially hungry but using so much magic lately was burning him up. He needed to eat more to keep up his strength.

Ulf set the tray down and said, "Lord Shenk, I didn't bring you a plate. Excuse me."

Otto waved him off and grabbed toast, a fried egg, and bacon, and made a sandwich. "This is fine. Believe me, after weeks in Rolan living off trail rations, anything home-cooked is welcome."

They ate in awkward silence and when they finished Otto said, "I need your expertise. It seems Markane is providing alchemy-based weapons to our enemies."

"I'm happy to provide any insight I can," Ulf said. "Please bear in mind that I was barely out of my apprenticeship when I was banished."

"Given that I know next to nothing about alchemy, you're probably the foremost expert in Garenland." Otto took the samples Axel provided out of his satchel and set them on the table. "Whatever's in the flask can prevent wizards from targeting whoever uses it. The second one is an explosive."

Ulf held the explosive jar up to the window so the light could shine through it. "I'm familiar with the dual-liquid explosive. As long as you have the ingredients, it's easy to make. You just shake the jar to mix them then throw. This sample is highly refined and very powerful. Whoever made it knows their business. Unfortunately, there's no way to counteract it beyond killing the person about to throw the missile or using magic to redirect it away from the target."

"And the other?" Otto asked.

Ulf unscrewed the flask's lid and poured a drop of silvery liquid that looked like mercury onto his hand. He rubbed the potion into both hands then held them up. "Try to attach a thread to my fingers."

Otto obliged, but the instant his thread got close, it vanished like smoke in the wind. He tried a heavier thread, one that should allow him to take Ulf's fingers off, and that one was destroyed as well.

"That substance is a nightmare," Otto said.

"Yes," Ulf agreed. "I've heard of mirrorshine, but never seen it. The anti-magic potion is very difficult to make. I wouldn't be surprised if this was made by Lord Valtan himself. The potion's only weakness is that the effects are temporary, a few hours at most. You can also target the space around the enemy and use the spell's secondary effects."

Otto was disappointed that there wasn't a way to directly counter the effects of the alchemical weapons, but at least there was a way to overcome them. "Hold your hands up again."

Ulf did as he asked and Otto spent a minute figuring out how close a thread could get before it dissolved. Four inches was plenty close enough to detonate a fireball and still blow someone's face off.

"Thanks for the information," Otto said. "Now I just need to figure out how to stop the prisoners from rioting."

"There I believe I can be of more help," Ulf said.

"You can?" Allen spoke for the first time since they finished breakfast.

"Yes. The item I was working on when I was banished is a drug that is highly addictive and causes tremendous pain during withdrawal. Should you get the miners hooked, they will be much easier to control. If you dose the evening meal, they'll be lethargic all night and should anyone misbehave, you can deny them the drug. Their screams will convince the others to not cause trouble."

Otto grinned. That was exactly what he needed. "How soon can you make a batch?"

"I'll need a day to prepare and supplies, fairly expensive supplies."

Otto pulled a heavy purse out of his satchel and thunked it down on the table. "That should buy whatever you need. This is your highest priority. I'll return in two days to collect the potion."

"What about us?" Sin asked. "We've been putting him off, but that wizard might start making demands."

"He's my next stop. I assure you, no demands will be forthcoming when I'm finished."

CHAPTER 13

After leaving the Thirsty Sprite, Otto's original intention was to head directly for the wizards guildhall, but halfway there he turned towards Franken Manor instead. Enoch had been a member of the wizard underground at one time. It couldn't hurt to see if he knew anything about the guild's intentions.

He found the old man sitting on a bench outside the barracks sipping tea and enjoying a sandwich. Since the last of the new recruits had completed their training, he hadn't had much to do. Otto wasn't sure what to do about that. At his age, traveling with the army wouldn't be a good idea. Besides, Enoch had never shown much in the way of killer instinct.

He noticed Otto approaching and shifted over to make room on the bench. "Back again. Will you be staying in Garen for a while?"

Otto sat and sighed. "No, too much is happening out in the empire. I'll be leaving again tomorrow or the next day, but right now I have a few issues here that need clearing up. I spoke to Sin and Allen this morning."

Enoch winced. "About the guild?"

"Indeed. I'm going to speak to Cypher shortly, but I wanted to talk to you first. You were part of the group years ago. Am I wasting my time? The underground was a great help taking the portals and the guild charter was their reward. I warned them not to try and force any wizards to join. It seems my warning fell on deaf ears. How does it look if I tell the wizards they're free then the guild shows up demanding they join?"

"Cypher and the guild mean well, Otto. I believe that with all my heart. Cypher was born in Tharanault and saw the worst of what ordinary people could do to wizards. He fears a return to those days and what will happen if we don't stand together. I told him it wouldn't matter. There aren't enough of us to defeat the combined forces of the world should they turn against wizards."

"You're quite right. Did your message get through?"

Enoch shook his head. "I don't think so. Even if it did with Cypher, he claims the guild master is pushing him and the other local guild representatives to bring the wizards around. He didn't say it out loud, but 'by any means necessary' was implied."

"I need this like I need a hole in the head." Otto stood. "Maybe I can arrange a meeting with the guild master. Have you met him?"

"Her and no I haven't. What little I've heard wasn't good. If you go that route, be careful. I know you're strong, but even you can't defeat a group of wizards on your own."

That depended entirely on how strong his opponents were and how numerous. "I appreciate the warning. If we meet, it will be on neutral ground. Rest assured, I don't intend to walk into a trap."

"It's the trap you don't anticipate that's dangerous. By the way, I saw your daughter, she's adorable."

Otto frowned. "Where did you see her?"

"Annamaria brought her out into the garden the other day when I was walking by. She seemed rather sad. You should spend more time with them. The empire's problems will still be there in a few days."

As if spending time with Otto would do anything to improve Annamaria's mood. "I appreciate the advice. I'll see if I can't find something more exciting for you to do."

Enoch waved him off. "Don't worry about me. I've reached the age where I can appreciate a little peace and quiet. Besides, you never know when a new recruit will show up."

That was true enough. Otto waved and took his leave. Even if it was a waste of time, he still needed to make sure Cypher understood that violence against wizards would be punished, severely.

⌒

The wizards guildhall was nothing to inspire anyone visiting. Through the front window, a young woman was visible. She sat at a small desk on the right-hand side of the front room, a book in her lap, seeming totally unaware of anything around her. At least Otto wouldn't have to wait in line.

The girl looked up when he entered and smiled. The bright expression was spoiled by a complete lack of straight teeth in her mouth. "Have you come to join the guild?"

"No, I've come to speak with Cypher."

"Uh, he doesn't usually—"

The back-room door opened and Cypher's scowling face

appeared in the gap. "It's fine. I've been expecting a visit from Lord Shenk. Please, join me in my office."

Otto nodded to the girl and strode into the back room. As offices went, at least it matched the rest of the building. Everything was plain but serviceable. Cypher sat behind his desk and gestured to one of the guest chairs. He didn't dress anything like you'd expect a wizard to. In his simple gray tunic and trousers, Cypher looked more like a workman than a mage. Though to be fair, Otto was probably closer to looking like a merchant than a wizard.

"I suppose you've spoken to Enoch," Cypher said when Otto had settled into his chair.

"Yes. Did I not make clear when I arranged for your guild to be recognized that no wizard would be forced to join? Beating them into obedience doesn't count as joining of their own free will."

"I haven't had anyone beaten," Cypher said.

"Only because all the thugs in this city answer to me and aren't stupid enough to do something that would force me to kill them. It certainly wasn't a lack of trying on your part. If this sort of thing continues, I'm going to have to revoke your charter."

"You can't!"

"Well technically *I* can't, but once I inform the emperor what you've been up to, I doubt he'll need much convincing to order the charter revoked."

"Wait. Please. I explained to Enoch why the guild is so important. Ultimately wizards can only trust each other. If you would just join us, you'd see how valuable the guild can be."

"I told you before, I answer to only one master and it isn't whoever runs this guild. I'm giving you one last chance. Tell your master and your fellow members that, from this day forward, if any wizard is troubled by your hand, directly or indirectly, you're done. Do I make myself clear?"

"Perfectly. I will relay your message to the guild master." Cypher's face twisted in a pleading look. "Won't you at least meet with her? Maybe the two of you could come to an understanding."

Otto smiled. He'd been hoping Cypher would make the offer. "Perhaps when I finish with other matters. For now, though, I feel I've been more than generous. Ignore this warning at your peril. You won't get another."

CHAPTER 14

Uther reached Split Rock late in the afternoon three days later than scheduled. The giant stone with a huge crack running down the center was a well-known place in Straken, but he doubted anyone outside the country knew about it. That was why he'd chosen it as their meeting place. Despite his late arrival, there was no sign of the Lady or more importantly the Markane weapons.

During his travels around Straken, he'd picked up two dozen volunteers, little more than boys really, who were eager to fight the enemy. He'd taken them on more out of desperation than because he thought they'd be much use in battle. At the very least they could throw an explosive jar. Or they would have been able to if the weapons had been here like they were supposed to be.

Where the hell could she be? He assumed they'd be here waiting and worrying. Instead, nothing. Something must have happened to them. Maybe they ran into a Garenland patrol. If she lost the weapons, Uther swore he'd kill her himself.

"We'll camp here tonight. Maybe the others will show up tomorrow."

Uther caught the eye of one of the rangers and nodded off to the side. "Majesty?" the ranger asked.

"Take a squad and look around. See if there's any sign the wagon made it this far. If they haven't, we'll need to backtrack toward Port White."

"As you command, Majesty." He collected nine men and they disappeared into the evening.

Uther would have complained some more if he thought it would help, but of course it wouldn't. Nothing had gone right since his father was taken. For a brief moment he'd dared to hope that the Markane weapons would turn the tide, but if he'd lost them, he didn't know what they were going to do.

He barely had time to toss his pack to the ground when shouts rang out. "Ambush!"

He reached for his sword just as dozens of Garenland soldiers came pouring into the clearing.

The rangers formed up quickly, their curved swords out and ready. Their foes weren't only scouts this time. Heavy infantry armed with spears and protected by mail armor and shields marched forward in their hundreds.

A cursory glance told him everything he needed to know. This wasn't a fight they could win.

"Disengage and withdraw!" Uther ordered.

He looked over his shoulder in time to see another force trotting down the road to cut them off. The enemy infantry formed up and pressed in, fully encircling the rangers.

A single man stood atop Split Rock. "Throw down your weapons and surrender. You can spend the rest of your life digging in the mines with your father."

Uther had seen that man before. He was the one that held

the dagger to his father's throat. The one he'd sworn revenge on. That seemed a dim possibility now.

"I'd rather die on my feet than in a hole chained up like a dog. Kill as many as you can!"

Uther charged at the nearest infantryman. He brought his sword down on the man's shield then was promptly shoved back.

A spear thrust creased his bicep.

All around was chaos. His men screamed and died as the Garenland infantry closed in, grinding them up like sausage meat.

This was not how Uther planned for his rebellion to end.

His enemies, unfortunately, had plans of their own.

He didn't have a chance to think before the rangers formed a ring around him and rushed the infantry wall. His men gave no thought to their own survival as they fought, dragging enemy soldiers down into the dirt.

Finally a gap appeared. One of the rangers shoved Uther through it and shouted, "Run, Majesty!"

A spear ran the brave man through.

His people were getting slaughtered and there wasn't a thing he could do.

No. There was one thing. He could honor their sacrifice. With his jaw clenched so tight it ached, Uther ran.

He angled toward the trees. He knew this land like he knew his own face. Night would fall soon. There was no chance the Garenlanders would catch him after dark.

Uther swore to every demon in hell that, somehow, he would make his enemies pay for what they had done.

Axel kicked a dead ranger over onto his back. He couldn't make out how the man had died in the twilight. Not that it mattered, dead was dead.

He'd been certain he had Uther this time. The rangers were surrounded, outnumbered, and taken by surprise. There was no way he could have failed. And yet when they made their suicidal charge on the shield wall somehow the rangers had forced a breach large enough for Uther to escape.

Maybe he shouldn't have held the wizards in reserve. All of them lacked experience in ambushes, at least that's how Axel justified his decision in his own mind. The truth was he still didn't really trust them. Besides, there was no guarantee Uther didn't have more of the magic blocking stuff.

The archers were another matter. The light had been failing, but still, his men were good enough that they could've taken Uther. Axel had wanted him alive. He wanted to see the son of a bitch chained up beside the king, his arrogant head bowed, in the deepest part of the mine.

He shook his head. None of it mattered of course. He'd failed, excuses be damned. At least they'd wiped out the rangers. On his own, Uther was no threat. Not that that meant he could just let the man go. His mission was to bring the prince in, dead or alive. They'd never get redeployed some-where, anywhere, but Straken, until that mission was complete.

His lips twisted in a bitter smile. When he found out, Otto would never let him hear the end of this.

"Sir?"

Axel turned at the sound of Colten's voice. "Give me good news."

"Sorry, sir. He reached the forest and it was too dark to see his tracks. I can easily pick up where we left off tomorrow if you want."

Axel nodded. The scouts would keep after him, at least for a few more days. He'd send the regulars back to Marduke. They'd done their job and done it well. Six dead and twenty wounded wasn't bad considering they'd taken down several hundred rangers.

"Let's make camp away from these corpses," Axel said. "We move at first light."

↻

Uther leapt from one tree to the next as he tried to throw the hunters off his trail. He couldn't see them or hear them yet, but he could feel the Garenland dogs nipping at his heels. They were back there somewhere, now that the sun had risen. Keeping to the trees was slowing him down but hiding his tracks in the rich loam of the forest floor was impossible. This was his only hope for escape.

And he would escape. He owed his men that after they sacrificed themselves to give him this chance. What he would do after he escaped was another matter altogether. He had no soldiers, no allies, and no hope of defeating Garenland, not now at least.

The only idea he'd come up with was to run to Port White and hope the Markane ship was still there. If anyone could help him, Lord Valtan could.

He spat the bad taste out of his mouth. How desperate was he, a Straken warrior, that he would look to a wizard for anything, much less securing his future? How did the saying go, desperate times and desperate measures? That particular saying could have been written just for this moment. He'd certainly never been more desperate in his life.

Eventually, Uther was forced to descend to the ground, mainly because he'd run out trees big enough to hold him. This part of the forest had been logged recently and the trees were little more than limby, ten-foot-tall scrubs.

Forcing his way through would take too long. Uther turned northwest, away from the trees, and jogged along the border between the new and old growth. The traveling was easy, but he could barely restrain a yawn. He'd been on his feet all night and leaping through the treetops took a lot more out of you than walking on the ground.

He refused to stop, at least not until he found somewhere he could lose his pursuers. Where the hell he was going to do that was another question altogether.

The answer came a little after noon. He emerged from the forest and hit a road. Fresh tracks littered it. A group of refugees, probably from Marduke, had come this way not that long ago. He stepped into the road and followed them.

An hour later he finally reached civilization. A small town of maybe a dozen buildings were clustered around an old stone well. Every house had a modest garden behind it and chickens were running free here and there. Uther debated turning away. He really didn't want to bring trouble on these people, but he needed help if he was going to survive. At a minimum food and somewhere to sleep for a few hours.

Taking a deep breath, he went to the first house and knocked. A woman appeared in the doorway, took one look at him, and pulled it the rest of the way open.

She lowered her head. "Your Majesty. How may I be of service?"

"I have a pack of Garenlanders on my trail. If you know a

place I can hide and could spare some food, you would have my gratitude."

"We have little enough, but I'm happy to share. One moment." She went into the house's back room and emerged a moment later with a heel of bread and some dried meat. "I fear it isn't much."

Right now, the food was the most delicious thing he'd ever seen. Uther devoured it in short order. "Thank you."

She bowed. "I would let you stay here, but I have nowhere to hide you. If you wish to rest, your best hope will be the Sharov farm a few miles out of town. He has many outbuildings where you could hide."

"Do you have a cart? I don't want to leave my tracks going to the farm."

She stared at him for a moment. "Would they know your tracks among all the others?"

"I fear they might. The Garenlanders have many skilled scouts. Perhaps I'm being overly cautious, but I would prefer not to take the chance." Uther didn't add that he wasn't sure he had strength enough to walk those final miles.

"As you wish, Majesty. I don't have a cart myself, but my neighbor does. She will let me borrow it."

"Please hurry. I don't know how far behind me they are."

She trotted off to the next house to the north. Uther didn't ask the woman's name, didn't want to know it. Should he be forced to talk, he didn't want to name her to the enemy. He owed her that at a minimum.

The two-wheeled cart she brought back looked barely sturdy enough to hold a basket of turnips. He feared if he stepped into it his foot would go straight through the rotten plank covering the floor. Fear or not, he didn't have much choice. Uther eased his weight onto the wood as gently as he could. The boards creaked but held.

He let out a slow breath and nodded. She took hold of the pull bar and set off. Uther crouched low, hoping no one else would notice him. Soon enough they left the village behind and followed a winding dirt track that eventually ended at the gate of a farm. Just as she said, there was one big main barn, five smaller sheds, and a house. For Straken, this was a massive operation. Most of the people worked small plots for their own use and either logged, trapped, or mined to make a living.

A solitary figure emerged from the main barn. His accomplice waved and called, "Mr. Sharov?"

He changed his course if not his pace and soon stood facing them from the opposite side of the three-rail gate. Uther rose so he could get a good look him and Uther could return the favor. The farmer looked like most of the people of Straken. Tall, muscular, weather-beaten face and simple, homespun tunic and trousers. The clothes didn't have any patches which marked him as relatively wealthy.

"Prince Uther?" Sharov asked. "What in heaven's name are you doing here?"

"It's a long story. The enemy is on my trail. I know it's a risk, but I need somewhere to rest and hide for the day. This fine lady suggested one of your outbuildings."

The farmer shrugged. "I don't mind. The curing shed is half full of bacon, but there's room for you in the back. It's not fancy by any means, but—"

"Anywhere out of sight is perfect, thank you. Tired as I am, I could sleep on a bed of rocks."

"Okay." Sharov opened the gate and led them back to a ten-by-ten shed. The smell of curing meat made Uther's mouth water and reminded him that he'd only had a few bites of food in over a day.

Uther ducked into the shed, turned back, and said, "Thank you both. I won't forget what you've done when we retake the kingdom."

Sharov closed the door and Uther worked his way to the back. There was a small clear area and he lay down. If he was found, there was no chance he could fight his way free of a large force. He found that oddly freeing and soon fell fast asleep.

CHAPTER 15

To say that Wolfric hadn't taken it well when Otto informed him of Markane's interference would be a vast understatement. He still held them partly responsible for his father's descent into perhaps not madness but something like it. He'd leapt at Otto's suggestion of a raiding force to keep them too busy to cause more trouble. Wolfric had even provided the names of several ship captains that were citizens of Garenland even though they sailed out of Lux.

With royal permission in hand, Otto had become one with the ether and traveled to Shenk Barony. The regular army was spread too thin to take even more soldiers away from their duties. Hopefully his father would see the benefit of providing troops in exchange for a share of the loot. Otto didn't care if they were garrison soldiers or mercenaries. As long as they had no compunction about killing.

He emerged from the ether fifty feet from the castle's front gate. With so many of his relatives inside Otto could hardly fail to arrive where he wanted to. He'd found that as long as he could get close to his target, he could shift the point where he appeared with no trouble. Lord Karonin hadn't mentioned being able to do that, but he assumed she considered it so obvious that it didn't need to be said outright.

He shook his head. That was the problem with dealing with someone that knew so much; they always assumed you knew more than you did. Either that or it was a test to see if he could figure out what to do on his own.

Speaking of his master, he should probably stop in and update her on his progress. He felt like he'd accomplished all of her demands, so she should be willing to reveal the next step to him becoming an Arcane Lord. If only there weren't a million other demands on his time, he'd be doing exactly that. Unfortunately, the empire was far too fragile right now to take however much time he'd need to complete the task.

As he strode up to the gate, the guards on duty snapped to attention. They all showed him a good deal more respect than they had when he was a child which made things considerably easier. As the portcullis clanked up Otto asked, "Is Father in?"

"Everyone is, my lord. Your brother returned only yesterday from a patrol. We've had hardly any trouble from bandits, thank heaven."

Otto echoed that sentiment. If he'd had to worry about bandits as well, he didn't know what he would have done. He ducked under the portcullis and headed straight for the keep. A quick glance at the training ring brought back many unpleasant memories. It seemed Graves didn't have anyone to torture today, poor fellow.

There was no guard outside so Otto pushed the door open himself. Despite it being early summer, a fire burned in the hearth. Father sat in front of it with his hounds at his feet. The dogs stood up and growled at Otto.

He ignored the beasts and focused on his father who finally got up from his chair. Baron Shenk remained an imposing figure in his black leather and fur-trimmed clothes. He would have looked right at home in Straken. The baron towered over Otto as he approached.

"What brings you here, boy?"

"Business. I have a proposal for you and Stephan. A military commission from the Crown."

"What sort of commission?" Father asked, his voice heavy with suspicion. Otto would have been offended, but his father was suspicious of everyone, so he didn't take it personally.

"A raid on Markane. You provide the manpower, I provide the ships, Stephan leads them, and we split the loot fifty-fifty."

Father snorted. "And who deals with Valtan, you?"

"No one. The Arcane Lord is bound to the capital. As long as the raid is confined to the outer islands, they'll be safe from his magic."

"Why not just send regular soldiers?"

"We can't spare them at the moment."

From behind Otto someone thumped down the steps. It was Stephan, his hair disheveled, feet bare, and dressed in a loose tunic and buckskins. "What are you doing here, runt?"

"I've come to offer you a job. Father and I are just working out the details."

"What sort of job?" Stephan dropped into a chair at the dinner table.

"That kind you're best at, looting, pillaging, and generally making life miserable for our enemies."

"Sounds like a lot of work," Stephan said.

"It'll get you away from Griswalda for a few months," Otto countered.

Stephan scratched his chin, clearly thinking it over.

"If you need us, I want sixty percent of the loot," Father said.

Otto had expected that. "You guarantee two hundred men and it's a deal."

"How long will the mission last?" Stephan asked.

"That depends on you. It'll last until either you get enough loot to fill the ships or Markane decides to make a deal with us to get you off their island. If you give it your all, I'd say three months at most."

"Deal," Father said, not looking at Stephan. "I can spare one unit from the garrison and I know a mercenary captain who'll jump at the chance."

"Good. Gather your people and meet me at the portal, shall we say in ten days?"

"Agreed." Father's stern expression cracked and he almost smiled. "I thought you'd be the most worthless of my sons and yet thanks to you Shenk Barony will be richer than ever. I knew arranging your marriage was a good decision."

Stephan licked his lips at the mention of Annamaria. Otto didn't bother getting upset. In fact, he would have happily given her to his brother if it wouldn't have destroyed the fiction he strove to maintain.

"Your mother is in her sewing room if you wish to speak to her before you leave." After that final pronouncement, Father strode out of the dining hall and turned toward his office. With the prospect of wealth in his eyes, Father would do his utmost to live up to the deal.

Otto took a step toward the stairs, but Stephan stopped him. "I never thought I'd see the day you'd ask anything from me. Don't think just because you threw this deal in Father's lap I've forgotten about what you did to me. I still plan to find that old wizard and cut his heart out."

So many changes in his life yet Stephan remained the same. He found that oddly reassuring. "If you find Master Enoch, he'll kill you. You should thank me for saving your life that day in the basement."

Otto stalked off before his brother could reply. He took the steps two at a time and soon stood in front of the door to his mother's sewing room. He knocked and a muted voice said, "Come in."

He pushed the door open and found his mother seated at her stitching frame. Her current project was a blanket embroidered with apple blossoms. It was very pretty. Everything Mother made was.

She stood and Otto hugged her. "What a nice surprise."

She stepped back and looked him all over. "You've lost weight. Aren't they feeding you enough?"

Otto chuckled. "Military rations aren't the tastiest. I've spent a lot of time in the field lately. Hopefully things will calm down soon."

He didn't see any need to mention that all the magic he'd been using was draining him as well. The last thing he wanted was to be a source of worry for his mother. Dealing with Stephan and Father was trouble enough and he wasn't even going to mention Griswalda.

"What are you working on?"

"A baby blanket. I was hoping to travel to Garen later this summer so I could spend some time with my new granddaughter. I'm sure Annamaria would like to have someone there to help lift some of the burden."

"There are lots of servants, but family is certainly best. We'll look forward to seeing you whenever you come."

Much as he loved her, Otto wasn't sure having his mother around would make his life any simpler. Even so, he'd be delighted to spend a few days with her. Trouble or not, his mother was easily the best thing he'd ever had in his life.

CHAPTER 16

Despite his best efforts, Colten lost Uther's trail in the forest about ten miles from the ambush site. The prince was headed northwest when they last saw his tracks and to Axel that meant only one possibility, he was making for Port White and the Markane ship anchored off the coast. Maybe Axel was right and maybe he was wrong, but either way he pointed his scouts in that direction and they marched hard.

Now they faced the wall surrounding Port White and happily found Garenland soldiers guarding it. General Varchi had taken Axel's advice and sent a garrison to occupy the town. Other than Marduke, Port White was the most important settlement in the kingdom, or province now that Straken was part of the new empire. They really should have seized control of the town long before now.

But done was done. Now that Garenland had control, there would be no more magical weapons coming through this way.

Axel marched up to the gate and a sergeant met him on the

opposite side of the heavy door. "Has anyone come or gone from the city in the past several days, Sergeant?"

"No, sir. The locals have been quiet as mice. We all figured this was going to be a tough post, but so far so good."

"Don't let your guard down. No matter how well behaved the locals are now, this is still Straken and any one of them would cut your throat without a second thought. What about the Markane ship?"

"She sailed south a few hours after we arrived. Not very friendly of them, but hardly surprising."

Axel scratched his chin. If the ship was gone, Uther would find no escape here, especially with the new garrison. But did Markane's vessel head for home or did they just find a new place to cause trouble? There were no more ports, but that meant nothing. They could anchor offshore and make landfall in any little cove they wanted.

"Is something wrong, sir?" the sergeant asked.

"Not exactly, it's just that my hunt suddenly got more complicated. Prince Uther was last seen headed this way. I doubt he'll be stupid enough to approach now that you're here but keep a close watch on anyone entering."

"Should we seal the town, sir?"

"No, if he's foolish enough to try and sneak in that's to our advantage. You can grab him, clap him in irons, and ship him off to Marduke."

"I'd hate to steal your glory," the sergeant said in a tone that suggested he didn't mean it.

Axel smiled. "Glory is for dead heroes. I want Uther caught, and I don't care who does the catching. Good luck."

"You too, sir."

"We're not going in?" Cobb asked.

"No point, what we want isn't there. What we need is a reliable local guide, someone who knows the best places to land a rowboat."

Cobb barked a humorless laugh. "You got a better chance of finding true love with a two-copper whore than a guide you can trust in Straken."

Axel couldn't argue with his second's observation. "What we really need is a lookout post. I mean how hard could it be to spot a huge, three-masted sailing ship?"

"How about a lighthouse?" Colten asked.

Axel spun to see the youthful scout pointing at a tall white tower sitting on a distant rock formation. It had to be fifty miles south of their position, but Axel saw no other options.

"Let's take a look."

○

Uther couldn't believe it. He stood in the trees and stared at Port White. The walls were crawling with men dressed in Garenland black and gold. They must have marched here immediately after the Lady in Red got caught. If the invaders had taken control of the town, he felt certain Markane's ship would be long gone. How the hell was he supposed to get out of here now?

He wanted to punch something, or better yet someone, preferably someone from Garenland. He took a deep breath to calm himself. Anger would only lead him into more trouble. He needed to think clearly. Just because the ship left Port White didn't mean they'd abandoned Straken altogether. There were tons of places they could make landfall in a small boat. Unfortunately, Uther knew the mountains better than he did the coast.

Some of the local fishermen could probably help him. They

were bound to notice a huge merchant ship sailing by. The nearest village was around thirty miles south of Port White. He sighed and set out, his over-used legs complaining bitterly.

For a day and a night he hiked southwest, careful to avoid the roads and resting only once in the crook of a knotty oak forty feet above the ground. Exhausted as he was, that had been as nice as a feather bed.

Now, a little past noon, he stood in the shadows of the trees watching a small fishing village. They had no wall or soldiers on patrol. There were a dozen cabins and just as many shacks down by the water. Nets, tools, and the remains of the day's catch filled the shacks. Of more interest to Uther were the ten small dories pulled up on the beach. If they knew where the Markane ship was, maybe Uther could get a lift out to it.

He was about to step out of the forest when he caught a glimpse of something dark moving among the cabins. Uther froze and watched. A moment later a Garenland soldier stepped into the gap between the cabins.

Some clever soul on the other side had the same idea as him. They were probably checking all the fishing villages. He'd have to wait until they left. Even Garenland didn't have enough soldiers to occupy every tiny village in Straken.

Sliding further into the trees, Uther dug out his last strip of jerky and started gnawing. The farmer that had sheltered him had also made a gift of dried meat and bread. Even though he seemed more prosperous than the rest of the villagers, offering extra food was a generous act, one Uther would remember when he returned to reclaim his birthright. And he would reclaim it. He refused to consider any other possibility.

For three hours the soldiers marched around. No villagers showed their faces. Probably wise of them. Uther had nothing but hate for the enemy, but they had proven largely willing to let noncombatants live unharmed and unharassed. Anyone putting up a fight, however, was dealt with mercilessly.

At last the patrol moved on. Uther waited a full hour to make sure they didn't either double back or leave a spy behind. When he was confident the village held no more enemies, he emerged from the forest and walked to the first cabin.

He knocked once and stepped back. After a long wait the rough-hewn door slowly opened. A man older than Uther's father peered out. His eyes widened and he opened up the rest of the way. "Your Majesty! It isn't safe. Please come inside."

"The enemy has gone, Grandfather, and I can't stay long. Has a ship sailed by in the past week or so, a large one?"

"Oh, yes. I saw the monster with my own eyes. Cursed thing nearly capsized me without so much as a 'how fare you?'"

"Do you know where it is now?"

"Aye, they anchored up a hundred yards off one of my favorite spots, scared the mackerel all off. Bloody merchants."

Uther smiled at the old man. Time had done nothing to harm his spirit. "I must ask a great favor. Though they may be rude, that ship is my only hope of escaping the men hunting me. Can you take me to where they're waiting?"

"Certainly, Majesty. Though I can't promise they're still where I saw them."

Uther waved a hand. "We'll deal with that should it become necessary. When can we leave?"

"Have to wait until first light. We'll never make it in the dark."

Uther's first instinct was to argue, but he knew next to nothing about the water. Best to trust in someone that had been doing this sort of thing for longer than he'd been alive.

◯

The march to reach the lighthouse Colten spotted left Axel exhausted. They'd arrived ten minutes ago, just in time to watch the sunrise. The lighthouse itself was abandoned and falling apart. Whoever ran the place had given up long before Garenland invaded.

Axel considered himself to be in pretty good shape, but two days of nonstop marching combined with only four hours' sleep had pushed him and the rest of his men to the brink of collapse. Had they been hunting a force of rangers, he would have ordered them to stop and rest, but even exhausted, the scouts should be able to handle Uther by himself. At this point the prince had to be as worn out as they were.

"There she is," Cobb said.

Axel forced himself to look. Sure enough, maybe half a mile off the coast, the Markane trader had anchored up. They hadn't even sailed that far from Port White. Arrogant bastards. Not that he could blame them. Markane was the only real sea power. The few warships Lux fielded were no match for them and the other kingdoms had even smaller fleets.

Now that they'd found the ship, Axel needed to figure out exactly what they were going to do about it. Their bows had no hope of reaching that far and he didn't know where Uther was going to meet them. Axel felt helpless and he hated that feeling.

"Anyone have any suggestions about how we might stop them?" Axel asked.

"Never a wizard around when you actually need one," Cobb muttered.

While Cobb grumbled, Colten eyed the ship and pulled his longbow. He couldn't possibly think he could hit it.

"I think I can hit it," Colten said. "We've got the advantage of height so if I aim high, I think I might just reach it."

Axel had no better ideas and it couldn't hurt to try. "Light your arrows and aim for the sails. Even all bunched up they should still catch. If we can burn those it might give us time to get a wizard out here to sink them."

Colten strung his bow while one of the other scouts prepared a flaming arrow. Flint and steel clicked and soon the rag was burning. Colten nocked the arrow and drew, aiming high. When he'd gotten the string drawn as far back as he could, he loosed.

Axel held his breath as the arrow arced out over the water. It slipped right between the masts, overshot the deck, and splashed into the water. Somehow, he'd reached the ship but missed the target.

"Another boat, my lord," Cobb said.

Sure enough, a fishing dory was making its way out to the Markane ship. Axel couldn't see any detail, but he refused to believe it was a coincidence. That had to be Uther.

"All archers break out your bows and fire at will. I want whoever's in that little boat dead. Colten, keep trying to light the big one on fire."

In short order arrows were arcing out toward the dory, all of them missing. Lacking a bow of his own, Axel could only watch and grimace at every missed shot. One arrow finally looked like it was going to take out the man at the tiller. A moment before impact, it hit an invisible barrier and bounced into the sea.

Axel turned to stare at the Markane ship. A solitary figure stood at the rear of the ship, hand raised. Demons take them! They had a wizard on that ship.

Two more accurate shots were turned away by magic. At

last the dory reached the merchant ship and a ladder was dropped. The person in the front of the boat, Axel assumed it was Uther though he couldn't prove it, climbed quickly up on deck.

"Save your arrows, men," Axel said. "They won this round."

All that time and chasing for nothing. Maybe it counted for a little that Uther was no longer in Straken to cause trouble, but that was cold comfort and Axel doubted the emperor would be pleased. Not to mention Otto.

"Let's pack it in, get some rest, and head to Marduke. For better or worse, this mission is finished."

CHAPTER 17

Otto emerged from the portal and was greeted immediately by a chorus of salutes from the guards. Everyone understood now that the portal would only open off schedule if he opened it. That was most helpful and assured no accidents from an overzealous archer. He waved them back to their positions and took a moment to look around.

The fort was complete. Fifteen-foot walls with a single gate controlled access to the portal. Watchtowers manned by archers marked each corner of the fort. A barracks had been built for the soldiers along with a storage building. Everything looked exactly as he expected which was a pleasant change of pace given what he'd walked into lately.

Satisfied with his brief inspection, Otto started for the gate. He made it halfway before Henry, the infiltrator he'd assigned to Lux, came jogging out of the barracks. More of a spy than an actual member of the garrison, he was dressed in plain civilian clothes.

He waved at Otto and said, "A moment please, Lord Shenk?"

"Henry, what do you need?"

"There've been some minor issues with the wizards. Two of them came to the fort to report being assaulted and their new shops vandalized. The criminals responsible made it clear that they needed to join the Wizards Guild unless they wanted more trouble."

Otto's jaw clenched. So they had started here as well. If that were the case, no doubt the guild would be up to similar tricks in the other provinces as well. He'd made the situation clear to Cypher, but perhaps he needed to be a bit more forceful.

"Do you know where the guild is based in Lux?"

"They have a building right here in Crystal City. I can show you."

"Excellent, lead the way."

Henry took off with Otto at his side. As they walked Otto asked, "Why didn't the wizards go to the city watch?"

"I can't say for certain, but I suspect the way they've been treated in Lux made them wary of the local law. And to be fair, Garenland is the true power here now. It makes sense that they'd reach out to us." Otto couldn't argue that. "May I ask what brought you to Lux, Lord Shenk?"

"Ships. I need two of them. The emperor mentioned that a handful of Garenland citizens moved here when relations were better and set up shipping businesses." Otto shook his head. "I can't imagine there was much call for that sort of thing when the portals were in full operation."

"Actually," Henry said. "For some of the coastal towns, it's faster to sail there directly rather than go through the portal then travel overland. Especially in Rolan and Straken given their size."

Otto raised an eyebrow.

Henry cleared his throat. "I've been trying to talk to as many people as I can to try and get a feel for the country. I spent a couple days down at the docks chatting with the merchants."

"Admirable. I wish all my subordinates were as conscientious in their work. When I'm finished at the guild, you'll have to guide me to the right people."

"It would be my pleasure." Henry pointed at a building across the street with a sign featuring an open book and wand. "That's the guild."

The door was closed and there wasn't a person in sight. Clearly their attempts at intimidation had failed to drum up any business. Good. Otto would have hated to see them benefit from such horrible behavior.

"Wait here." Otto crossed the street and knocked on the open door.

As he waited, he charged his body with ether. It finally opened and a man in his early thirties looked out. His eyes widened when he saw Otto.

And that was the last thing he saw. Otto's fist crashed into the man's face and sent him staggering back before he collapsed on the floor.

The noise drew the attention of someone in the back room. A second door opened and a woman demanded, "What's going on out here?"

"I was giving your associate an explanation as to why violence is a bad way to convince people to do what you want. For example, it's hard to negotiate with someone who's unconscious. Since you're awake, I'll talk to you."

"Who the hell do you think you are?" She sent five threads charged with lightning at him.

Otto brushed them aside and moved closer. "My name is Otto Shenk. I've already had this conversation with Cypher in Garen. It seems he neglected to pass the warning on, so I'll tell you what I told him. Leave the wizards alone. If they want to join your guild, fine. I don't care one way or the other. But if I hear any more of them have been attacked, I'm going to come back here and rip your head off. I suggest you pass this warning on to your fellow guild leaders. If I hear one more complaint, someone's going to die."

"You think you can come in here, threaten us, and just walk away?"

She had guts; Otto had to give her that. He drew his mithril sword and placed the tip at her throat so fast she didn't have time to blink.

"I don't have to walk away. And neither do you. You people and your precious guild are causing me trouble I don't need. The only reason I don't wipe you out is because you were helpful in seizing the portals. Whatever goodwill you earned is gone. Tell me, do I walk away or do we finish this fight?"

She swallowed hard. "Perhaps I was rash. If Cypher hasn't spoken to the guild master, I will. I will also send messages to the other halls. Rest assured, there will be no more trouble."

"Good. That's exactly what I wanted to hear." Otto sheathed his blade and without another word marched back out of the guildhall.

"Is all well, my lord?" Henry asked when he rejoined the spy outside.

"Time will tell. Withdraw whatever you need from the portal guard's funds to pay for the wizards' damaged shops. I'll replace the money when I get back to Garen. Now, let's head to the docks. I have ships to hire."

Happily, the docks were only a ten-minute walk from the

guildhall and the streets were quiet save for the occasional well-dressed person on their way here or there. Half a dozen ships waited at the end of the wharfs, none of them huge, but all big enough to carry a hundred men to Markane and plenty of treasure back. Still, he thought there'd be more.

"Is this all?"

"Most of the fleet is out fishing," Henry said. "Another handful are delivering merchandise. This is actually a pretty good selection for this time of year. The two you want are over there. Both captains were born in Garenland and I suspect that's where their true loyalty lies."

Otto strode over to the first ship he indicated and stopped in front of the gangplank. "Hello? Anyone on board?"

A few seconds later a bearded, scowling man in a blue canvas outfit stalked up to the railing. "Who wants to know?"

"Otto Shenk. I'm looking to hire a pair of ships on Crown business. My companion tells me the captain of this ship is a Garenlander by birth. Would that be you?"

"Ayup. What's the job?"

"Troop transport, from here to one of the Markane outer islands and back. We'll pay a ten percent cut of the loot for the ship."

"How soon do you want to set sail?"

"Depends on how long it takes to gather our soldiers. Two weeks or so."

"I have no pressing business. I accept your commission. Name's Captain Wainwright and we'll be ready when you are."

Otto nodded, pleased to have secured his first ship. Rare as it was, things did occasionally go right.

He didn't trust that for a moment.

CHAPTER 18

No thugs waited outside the Thirsty Sprite when Otto approached in the early afternoon. Sin probably couldn't get anyone to stand guard anymore. It was a pity he'd had to move the former king and his daughter into the Crow's Nest, but he needed somewhere safe to keep them under close watch and in reasonable comfort. He knew of nowhere else that fit the bill.

What they really needed was a proper base for the intelligence network. Somewhere big enough for a real alchemy lab, a dungeon, an armory, and space to store the magical armor. Otto shook his head. He'd add finding such a place to the list of a million other things he needed to do.

When Otto knocked today, Allen opened the door promptly. "Lord Shenk. I assume you're here to pick up that horrible concoction Ulf's been cooking in my kitchen. Come in."

Otto entered the nearly empty tavern. There was no sign of Sin. No doubt the acrid stench filling the place had driven her out. Hard to believe anything that smelled like that could be good for causing euphoria. Maybe finding a new base needed to move up the priority list.

"Where's your lovely comrade in arms?"

"Sin took off ten minutes after Ulf got started. She said she'd find somewhere else to work until he finished. I shut the tavern down as well. We told everyone there were rats and the stink was poison."

"I imagine that will do wonders for your business."

Allen shrugged. "My regulars aren't the fussy sort. They'll just be happy there are no rats."

"No troubles to report?"

"None. According to Sin, the Wizards Guild hasn't made any further attempts to hire muscle. I've heard nothing about spies or sabotage. Garen is enjoying a rare quiet spell and I'm not complaining."

"Nor me." Otto nodded to himself. "If we have some quiet, this might be a good time to properly set up. A tavern was fine when we were getting started, but now we need more. I want you to find a space, something in the industrial area where the stench won't draw attention. It needs to be big enough for you, Sin, and Ulf to operate out of with room for storage. Lots of storage."

"What's my budget?" Allen asked.

"Find the right building. Price is irrelevant. I'll get the money from the Crown if I can't get it from my father-in-law. If you can't convince the current owner to sell, I'll talk with them."

"Got it. Timeline?"

"As soon as possible. If Ulf's stuff works, I want him set up to produce more, quickly."

"I'll start looking today."

Before Allen could say anything else, the kitchen door

opened and Ulf emerged along with a cloud of steam. "The first batch is ready."

Otto left Allen and joined Ulf in the doorway. "Let's see."

The kitchen had been transformed into a lab, complete with scorched glass beakers, tubes, and burners. Turning it back into a kitchen wasn't going to be quick or easy. Not that Otto cared. At this point, they didn't need a cover. Allen could close the tavern altogether for all it mattered.

On the counter sat a steel container shaped like a small bucket with a heavy lid tightly clamped on top. Ulf placed a hand on the container. "Here it is. Enough of the drug to enslave thousands for a month. Mix one teaspoon to five gallons of liquid. Water, alcohol, even soup or stew will work. Just make sure whoever is preparing the mix doesn't get any of the raw drug on bare skin. The result would be bad."

"How bad?"

"Raving madness followed by massive heart failure within thirty minutes."

"That's certainly bad." Though Otto could also imagine plenty of uses for it as a poison. "Allen's going to get you set up in a proper lab away from here. As soon as you're ready, get the next batch started. Do you need money?"

"I have enough with what you gave me for a second batch. After that I'll need more."

Otto nodded. He'd need to set up a steady source of funds for their operation. Though given his resources that should pose no problem.

"Lord Shenk, I can't tell you how wonderful it feels to be doing the work I was trained for. Mixing drinks is a poor substitute for true alchemy."

Otto grinned. "If I can ever scare up an afternoon off, I'd

very much like to observe the process. My understanding of alchemy is limited and I'd like to fix that."

"Any time. I would be delighted to show you what little I know." Ulf offered a deep bow.

Otto collected the drug and turned to leave. The sooner he delivered the drug, the better. Dead prisoners didn't produce after all.

○

Traveling through the ether had spoiled Otto. After arriving in Marduke, he spent a day and a half riding north to the mines along with a group of soldiers headed that way to relieve the guards on duty. Axel, unfortunately, was off somewhere hunting Prince Uther so Otto couldn't just use their connection to appear at the mine.

Maybe he should make a safe room and rune mark it to save time. He dismissed the idea as quickly as it appeared. Rune marking the mine implied that he would be visiting often and that was the last thing he wanted. Otto could easily find scores of better uses for his time than dealing with the mines.

Speaking of the mines, the exterior fortifications had been rebuilt and reinforced since the attack. The stone walls were now over ten feet high and nearly that thick. A pair of towers allowed the archers a good field of fire. All in all, Otto was impressed. They'd accomplished a lot in a short time. That showed initiative which he liked. Too many officers liked to sit on their asses and do the minimum. Whoever took over from Axel clearly wasn't that sort.

Otto dismounted in the courtyard inside the wall. The mine entrance resembled a tunnel into hell, the darkness broken only by a red Lux crystal. A group of soldiers emerged from the tunnel along with an officer with lieutenant's symbols on his black and gold uniform.

He spotted Otto and hurried over. "Lord Shenk. We didn't have word you were coming. My name is Baldwin, I currently command this post."

"No need for any fuss. I've brought what I hope will be a solution to your rioting problem."

"Heaven's blessing on you, sir. If you have some way to keep these savages in line, I would welcome it and so would my men."

Otto pulled the container out of his mount's saddlebag. "This is filled with a magical concoction that will induce a state of euphoria in the prisoners. Mix it with their food at night and they'll give you no trouble before morning. Should there be a problem, withdraw the potion and tell them the offenders are to blame. The pain will quickly remind them why they should do as they're told. It might take a few weeks to get them properly trained, but after that I doubt you'll have any more trouble."

"We'll try anything," Baldwin said. "The prisoners riot several times a week. It's as if they want us to kill them."

"Given that your prisoners are from Straken, that might be the truth. If you'll escort me to your cook, I'll instruct him on how to prepare the dose."

Otto followed his guide down into the darkness. It was a short walk to the side chamber that served as a barracks for the soldiers on duty. Behind it was a simple kitchen with a huge kettle bubbling over the fire.

A surly looking bearded man in a stained white short-sleeve tunic looked up as they entered. He offered a half-hearted salute. "Sir?"

"Lord Shenk has a special ingredient you will be adding to

the prisoners' food. Pay close attention to his instructions."

Otto passed on the directions Ulf had given him. When he finished, he added, "Make sure not to get any in the soldiers' food as it is highly addictive."

The cook accepted the drug container. "If it keeps those slobs from complaining about my stew it'll be worthwhile."

Otto was about to take his leave when a gong sounded deeper in the mine.

"Not again," Baldwin muttered. "It's a riot. Excuse me, Lord Shenk, but I need to deal with this."

"Perhaps I can be of assistance," Otto said. "Lead the way."

Baldwin thankfully saw no need to try and dissuade him and the two men made their way quickly down a sloping tunnel. It branched first to the left then the right. They went right and Otto soon heard shouts and the clash of steel.

"Ahh!" A man dressed in rags and manacled hand and foot shuffled toward them, a pickax raised above his head.

Baldwin went for his sword, but Otto struck first. A weak bolt of lightning set the prisoner on his backside. He wouldn't be getting up again for a while.

"Well struck, my lord. I wish we had more ways to put them down without killing them."

They hurried on and soon reached a wall of soldiers armed with shields and batons facing a gang of prisoners armed with pickaxes. Both sides flailed at each other to little effect. The prisoners' bindings worked with the narrowness of the tunnel to limit their attack options.

Otto sent thirty targeting threads into the first two rows of prisoners. A weak pulse of lightning dropped them in one go.

The prisoners behind them stopped cold. No doubt seeing so many of their fellows taken down with a single shot knocked the fight out of them.

"Back to your work or you can join them!" Baldwin shouted.

At the rear of the group Otto spotted King Uther watching closely. Looked like the old man had some spirit left. That wouldn't do at all.

"Lieutenant, kindly grab the former king and bring him somewhere he and I can have a private chat. I have a strong suspicion that he's the cause of at least some of your problems."

"As you command, Lord Shenk."

The private location Baldwin brought him to was basically a cave just off the main tunnel. A few crates of supplies sat in one corner but otherwise it was empty. Uther glared at him across the empty space. His hands were manacled behind his back to keep him from trying anything. Not that Otto was overly concerned about a single old man whose best days were behind him, but he appreciated Baldwin's thoroughness.

"I don't know what you have to say, but I'm not interested," Uther said. "Kill me or send me back to my men."

"I am going to send you back," Otto said. "But first I need to make a few modifications to your behavior. The constant riots are a bother and I'm certain you're responsible. Not that it takes much agitating, you are men of Straken after all. I expect you to act like savages."

"And you are an arrogant, condescending Garenland fop. If you think you can modify my behavior, you're dreaming."

Otto flicked his ring and bound Uther in place, eyes open. "I never considered myself much of a fop. I prefer comfort to fashion. Now bear with me. I've gotten better at this, but I still have a long way to go."

He conjured the wheel of color in front of Uther and started it spinning. Once he was fully entranced, Otto said, "Whenever you think of lashing out at your captors, you will instead pinch the side of your right arm. Whenever one of your men suggests something violent, you will be struck with a blinding headache that won't go away until you convince them to stand down."

Otto repeated his commands over and over until a thread of ether inserted into Uther's brain showed the suggestions had taken hold. That addition to the programing spell was a wonderful help. He wished he'd had something similar when he was working on Lothair.

When the task was completed, Otto released Uther and stepped back.

"I told you," Uther said. "You won't control me with your cheap magic."

Otto waited a moment then Uther reached down and pinched the side of his arm. Grinning, Otto said, "I guess you showed me. Baldwin! You can return His Majesty to the company of his fellow prisoners."

Between the drug and Otto's suggestions, he felt confident that the worst of the mine problems should be in hand. With that done, he became one with the ether and returned home. With any luck, Stephan would be in Garen soon.

CHAPTER 19

Otto watched as a modest military force marched through the portal guard fortress. The guards on duty kept a close watch but remained silent. He never would have thought it possible, but for the first time in his life, he was happy to see his eldest brother.

Stephan arrived in Garen a day early and at the head of a force of two hundred of the most brutal-looking soldiers Otto had ever seen. Not the garrison unit of course, they were all dressed in the standard Shenk uniforms over mail coats. They each carried a sword, shield, and laden pack.

The mercenaries were another matter altogether. They wore no uniforms and carried no standard weapons. Each person, both men and women, carried whatever weapon they liked, from axes to shortswords to longbows and crossbows.

Stephan stood at the head of the procession, his thin blond hair corralled by a steel helm. A solid steel chest plate augmented his mail coat and a longsword hung at his hip. Beside him, a shorter man with a darker complexion and greasy hair chewed a wad of tobacco. He wore only heavy leather armor and carried a pair of hand axes tucked into his belt.

Otto tried not to let his distaste show. These people were going to slay his enemies, not spend the night at Franken Manor. As long as they could fight, nothing else mattered.

Stephan took a deep breath and looked up at the portal. "It's been too long since I visited the city. Pity there's no time to visit the whorehouses."

"Charming as always, Stephan. I've arranged your ships and supplies. If you're ready, we can head directly to Lux."

Stephan eyed the portal with a good deal less enthusiasm. "This is safe, isn't it?"

"I keep forgetting, this is your first time traveling by portal. Rest assured thousands of people have come and gone through here." Unable to resist, Otto asked, "You're not afraid, are you? Axel didn't even flinch when he went through."

"I'm not afraid of anything," Stephan snarled. "But if you wanted to get rid of me and make it look like an accident, this might be a good way."

Otto shook his head. Did Stephan have any idea how much power he'd have to give up to become a baron? Probably not. Knowing Stephan, he probably figured whatever he had was the best thing around and everyone else was jealous and wanted to take it.

"If it makes you feel better"—Otto pulled out the control rod and charged it with ether—"you can go last."

He touched the portal and ether roared through it. When the opening was filled Otto gestured "after you."

Stephan bared his teeth and stomped through, followed quickly by the rest of the soldiers. Otto followed them. The ether streamed around him and an instant later he stepped out into the Lux fort. Otto had sent a message earlier in the week letting them know the force was coming. He didn't want anyone panicking and doing something stupid.

Otto deactivated the portal and led the way through the fort's gate. It was a few minutes' walk to the docks and when they arrived they found Henry and Captain Wainwright standing at the foot of one of the two vessels' gangplanks.

Henry hurried over and bowed. "Lord Shenk, everything has been prepared as you ordered. The wizards are already aboard. If everyone else will join them, you can sail with the tide."

"Excellent, Henry, thank you." Otto turned to his brother. "You'll find food and other supplies on board. Once you've made landfall, I'll try and check in at least once a week. If you have any questions or need anything extra, now's the time to speak."

"What's this about a wizard?" Stephan asked. "I need no spell flingers getting underfoot. Steel and fire will see this done."

"Not wizard, wizards, four to be precise, two per ship. They're not here to help you, their job is to protect the ships from any Markane naval vessels that might show up. You'll have a hard time bringing your loot back if your transport is at the bottom of the ocean."

Stephan grunted and turned to the mercenary captain. "Let's load them up."

Otto watched the group divide into two and march up the loading ramps. Stephan followed his men without a word to Otto. Exactly as expected.

Henry eased closer and in a low voice said, "Your brother is... interesting."

"Stephan's a monster. A murderous, black-hearted brute who takes pleasure only in hurting others. Sending him to

Markane is the best way I could think to punish them for aiding our enemies."

"That's rather harsh, my lord. He's still your family."

"Yes, lucky me. On a more important note, has there been any more trouble with the Wizards Guild?"

"No one's complained and I've heard nothing about violence, so I assume not."

"Good, maybe the message got through this time."

CHAPTER 20

Otto set aside a report that just came in from Straken and leaned back in his chair. Apparently, Prince Uther had escaped Axel aboard a Markane ship, the same one that brought in the alchemical weapons. It seemed Valtan was planning to grant him asylum in Markane. That actually suited Otto fine. If Uther was in Markane, he wasn't running around causing trouble in Straken. Dead would be better; out of the way sufficed, for now at least.

He smiled to himself. It would be amusing if Uther ran into Stephan and got himself killed. To escape Axel and die at the hands of his brother, the irony was too much to hope for. A quick review of the various hot spots made it clear that, for the moment, nothing demanded Otto's attention. He was finally free to indulge himself.

Today that indulgence would take the form of exploration, specifically the tunnels near Lasil. If the Wizards Guild was interested in the place, there had to be something worth checking out. Besides, maybe he could get some kind of an idea about their intentions. Assuming they had any beyond representing all the empire's wizards. That was one plan that was never going to come to fruition. Not while Otto was alive anyway.

He stood, collected his mithril sword, belted it on, and became one with the ether. Otto shifted south, keeping his awareness focused on Lord Karonin's magical signature. If she made those tunnels and used them with any frequency, there had to be a rune mark allowing her to come and go.

At first, he was dragged toward the armory, but he fought the pull and soon felt another energy source. This one was at least in the correct direction. Otto willed himself to it and an instant later appeared in a pitch-black, silent space. He concentrated, trying to detect anything that might be a threat.

He could have been alone in the world for all he could tell.

Otto agitated the ether to create a light and got his first look at the chamber where he appeared. He stood on a raised platform with one of Lord Karonin's runes carved into the surface. The rest of the cavern was nothing but smooth rock with a single tunnel leading out.

At the end of the exit tunnel was a massive cavern. It had to be at least a quarter mile across and a hundred yards to the ceiling. This must be the nexus chamber his agent mentioned.

Otto stared in awe for a moment. He couldn't even imagine the power and time it must have taken to carve something like this out of solid stone under the ocean. It reminded him once more how far he had to go to equal his master.

Just to be on the safe side, he extended his sight for a quick look around. If some of the guild members were here, he didn't want to stumble into them. The nearest tunnel to his right led to another nearly empty cavern. Only some broken wood and debris covered the floor.

The next chamber was filled with light and a trio of figures dressed in tan robes stood around a hole in the floor surrounded by runes. It looked very much like the flesh warping chamber he found in Straken. Perhaps Lord Karonin conducted more dangerous experiments down here. That would explain the location.

One of the wizards, a woman with pale eyes, looked up and stared at Otto's ethereal eye. He dissolved it at once and started walking toward the tunnel leading to the wizards. They knew he was here, so he saw no reason to hide. Better to make it clear who was master of this place.

He didn't even make it to the tunnel entrance before the guild wizards appeared at the entrance.

"Who are you and what are you doing here?" the woman asked. "This complex is the property of the Wizards Guild. I don't know how you found your way down here, but you can find your way back out. Now."

"My name is Otto Shenk and this complex belongs to the empire as does everything else on or under the continent. Barring orders from my emperor, I go where I like, when I like, within it. Now, that pit you three were staring at in bewilderment seemed interesting. I believe I'll take a closer look."

The three wizards made no move to get out of his way. Disappointed but hardly surprised, Otto put a hand on his sword and infused his body with ether. Next he formed a shield around himself.

Not a moment too soon. Two targeting threads and a binding enchantment streaked out and shattered on his shield.

Since they made the first aggressive move, he felt free to counterattack.

In the blink of an eye he closed on the right-hand wizard. A hard blow to the stomach doubled him over and collapsed his knees.

A straight right to the jaw dropped the second man like a sledgehammered steer.

Otto spun and rested the edge of his sword on the woman's neck. Whatever spell she was attempting died half formed.

"Now, what do you say we end this foolishness while you're all still breathing?"

"Very well," she said with a faint tremor in her voice. "I'll ignore your intrusion this once, but if you wish to return, please get the guild's permission first."

Otto smiled as he returned his sword to its sheath. "Yes, I'll be sure to do that."

He made his way down the tunnel with the woman at his heels. The walk to the pit took less than a minute. When he arrived, there was no musty odor like he remembered from the Straken pit. Perhaps Lord Karonin didn't work on furry animals here. The pit itself was empty and totally clean.

The runes around the rim looked very similar to the ones at the first site. He'd have to check his notes to be sure, but Otto was confident there wasn't much difference.

"We can't make heads or tails of those markings," the woman admitted.

Otto didn't know exactly what they meant even though he understood the pit's function. His master had yet to teach him about flesh shaping. He assumed when she did, the runes' purpose would be part of the lesson.

When he'd satisfied his curiosity, Otto retreated back the way he'd come past the male wizards, one of whom was still unconscious and the other who was trying to make it to his feet and failing miserably.

As he turned toward the next tunnel the woman said, "What are you doing?"

Without breaking stride, he said, "Continuing my tour, what does it look like?"

"Did you not understand? This is our territory. You're neither wanted nor welcome."

Otto glanced back. "I understand perfectly. I simply don't care. If you're not going to try and stop me, I'd appreciate it if you'd shut up so I can concentrate."

He sensed no attack coming so at least she was smart enough to recognize she was outclassed. The woman hurried up to walk beside him. "If you're going to do this, I at least need to keep an eye on you."

He had no idea what she hoped to accomplish by that, but her presence didn't bother him either way. "What's your name?"

"Esmay. I've been studying this complex for over a year and I don't appreciate you poking your nose in."

"Have you learned anything useful?" Otto asked.

"I... That's none of your business."

"I'll take that as a no." Otto turned down the next tunnel.

The tunnel ran about the same distance as the last one and ended in a chamber filled with tables, chairs, four cots and matching footlockers.

"Our living quarters," Esmay said. "Hardly a ground-breaking discovery."

She was a spunky thing, he had to give her that. The way she acted made him think she was younger than him even though he guessed her age to be at least five years his senior. Given all Otto had done, he often felt older than his eighteen years. At this point he at least had everyone in Garenland trained to treat him with the respect he deserved. Mostly anyway.

He spent the next couple hours checking the rest of the

tunnels but found nothing interesting. The shaping pit was the only thing of note in the complex. Otto couldn't imagine his master had built this place for something so small, but he was certain she had her reasons.

Esmay guided him to the tunnel that led up to Lasil. "You know the way out. Feel free never to return."

With that final goodbye, she turned and marched off.

Otto shook his head. He so seldom ran into pleasant, agreeable women in his travels. He actually found he was missing Corina. At least she had been keen to learn and didn't insult him. Maybe he'd pay a visit to Rolan and see how things were going. There hadn't been any reports of further attacks, but that didn't necessarily mean all was well.

CHAPTER 21

Stephan had never traveled by ship before and he hoped to only have to do it one more time. The rolling and heaving left him sickened for three days before he finally got used to the motion. That wasn't as bad as some of his men, but it was bad enough.

Now at least he could stand at the rail and not want to empty his stomach into the sea. On the horizon, the western-most of Markane's outer islands was getting bigger by the moment. After the miserable trip, Stephan was ready to kill someone, preferable several someones.

"My lord?" Captain Wainwright said. "If you wish to prepare your men, we'll be at the anchorage in about an hour and a half."

"We're not going right to their docks?" Stephan asked.

"They're not deep enough for a ship our size. The only place we could dock is the capital and none of us wants to go anywhere near there. We put on extra-large longboats for this trip. We can land you all in four trips. I've selected a secluded beach a mile west of the nearest town. It'll be an easy mark once you're ready."

Stephan didn't care for the idea of being out on the water exposed to enemy arrows with no protection, but if they were far enough away from any people it should be okay. Besides, it didn't seem like he had much choice.

"Do what you must, Captain. The sooner I'm off this ship, the happier I'll be."

Captain Wainwright nodded and returned to his place at the ship's wheel. Stephan pushed away from the rail and clattered down the narrow steps to the lower deck. A pair of Lux crystals illuminated the hold which had been converted to carry people rather than cargo. Not that anyone did much beyond hanging up hammocks, but whatever, they made the trip safely and that was what mattered.

Most of the mercenaries were sitting on the deck in small groups playing dice or cards. Stephan's own troops were polishing their swords and armor. The moment they spotted him, the guards leapt to their feet.

"We'll be making landfall soon," Stephan said. "Whatever preparation you need to make, I suggest you make them. I want everyone on deck and ready for battle in one hour."

He caught the eye of the mercenary captain, Jost, and nodded off to one side. The scarred warrior joined him and raised a bushy eyebrow. "My lord?"

Stephan told him the captain's intentions then said, "I was thinking we should have everyone keep a shield handy. I doubt there'll be trouble, but better to take precautions."

Jost nodded. "I'll spread the word. Do we march on the town immediately or wait until morning?"

"Immediately. If they have lookouts posted, someone is bound to see our ship. I don't want to give them a chance to set a trap. Besides, a warm bed with a warm woman in it would suit me very well after all this time at sea."

Jost smiled. "Likewise. I assume the havoc order still stands?"

"Of course. My brother wants the islanders to suffer and I'm happy to oblige. Try to keep your men from burning too much. We want roofs over our heads for the night and torched loot isn't worth much."

"No need to worry, my men know their business. That's why your father hired us after all."

Stephan assumed his father hired them because they were the cheapest mercenaries around, but if they knew what they were doing that was a nice bonus.

⌒

Stephan wasn't sure if the people of Markane were arrogant or just stupid. As he and his mercenaries approached the nearest town, he couldn't help noticing that they didn't even have a low palisade or watch towers to offer archers a vantage point. Had they really been at peace for so long they couldn't even imagine being attacked?

He shrugged and eased his sword out of its sheath. People were visible outside. One woman, a pretty one, was hanging clothes out to dry. A boy chased chickens back toward a coop. No guards or soldiers were visible.

Jost looked his way and Stephan motioned for him to take half the men around to the far side of the town. Wouldn't want any of their catch escaping after all.

He gave the mercenary five minutes then straightened and yelled, "Havoc!"

Mercenaries roared and charged into the peaceful village

with Stephan at the front.

His first strike split the boy chasing chickens nearly in half. Warriors fanned out and screams soon filled the air.

Stephan found his next target, a stout man charging with a hoe raised above his head. Pathetic.

A cross parry batted the makeshift weapon aside and Stephan finished him with a thrust through the guts.

Leaving the man to bleed out, he stalked between a pair of freshly whitewashed cottages and emerged in the town center. All around, soldiers were hacking down unarmed villagers.

It was a slaughter plain and simple.

And that was fine. Stephan wasn't looking for a challenge, only loot and victory. He'd met fighters over the years that weren't satisfied by anything less than fighting an opponent that pushed them to the very edge of death. He had always assumed they had nothing worth living for and so wanted an honorable suicide. As a future baron, Stephan had everything to live for, assuming you overlooked his wife.

Ten minutes after they arrived, Jost came running up. "That's that."

A dozen young women, including the one he'd spotted earlier hanging up laundry, were being herded toward the center of town. Stephan licked his lips. That was very good indeed. They were the only survivors and by the end of the night, they'd envy the dead.

"Do you think they'll all be this easy?" Jost asked.

"No. Eventually what passes for an army on this miserable island will be dispatched to find us. Tell the men they can have their fun after they check the buildings for anything of value."

"And where will you be?" Jost asked.

Stephan nodded toward the laundry woman. "Advantages of leadership."

CHAPTER 22

Cypher arrived at the Hidden Hall three days after the guild master's summons reached him. The three-story tower, hidden by a perfect illusion, always gave him the shivers. The halls were dark, only Cypher's conjured light dispelled the gloom. Since an illusion kept anyone from seeing it, you'd think Lord Karonin would have added some windows.

Over the years he'd explored much of the building. There was a library and storage rooms filled with magical paraphernalia they couldn't begin to identify.

As he approached the double doors that led to the meeting hall, Cypher pushed all other thoughts out of his mind. Now was not the time to be distracted. He'd been expecting and dreading a summons ever since his first and only conversation with Otto Shenk. What he didn't know was what the guild master intended to do about the powerful young nobleman. He'd made it perfectly clear that he had no intention of joining the guild or letting them force others to join.

Cypher sent ether into a rune beside the door and when it

began to glow, the doors swung open. Inside, a dark, rectangular table dominated the space. At the head of the table sat a figure in voluminous gray robes. A hood hid the guild master's face.

Cypher went to his assigned spot and bowed. "Guild master. Have the others arrived?"

"Yes, you're the last." Her voice was surprisingly deep and husky. "Tell me about him."

She didn't need to elaborate. "What do you want to know?"

"Can he be convinced to join us? Is there anything we can offer?"

Cypher licked his lips. "I don't think so. He made it perfectly clear to me that his only loyalty is to the emperor. I believe he feels that even if he wanted to join the guild, it would be impossible to divide his loyalty."

"Admirable if inconvenient. As our third-strongest member, could you defeat him in a duel?"

"I don't know his skill level well enough to say for sure but given what he's accomplished in such a short time, I doubt it."

"Fair enough. I'll summon the others."

It took only five minutes for the rest of the guild leaders to join them. When everyone had taken their assigned place the guild master said, "You know why we're here. The question of Otto Shenk must be answered. If he won't join and refuses to allow us to compel others to join, our guild will die before it's born. I open the floor to you all."

"Why are we even debating this?" said a tall, broad-shouldered man that would have looked more at home as a knight than a wizard. Tal of Tharanault was never one to mince words. "We should kill him as a warning to anyone else that would dare oppose us. We eliminate an obstacle and send a message all at once. Simple."

"There's a problem with that," Cypher said. "If we kill him and make it clear that we did, I doubt the emperor will take that quietly. Unless we're ready to go to war with the entire continent, I suggest a less aggressive approach."

"I second that," the ancient old woman that served as Rolan's leader said. Cypher couldn't remember hearing her called anything but Grandmother. "Considering what that boy did for the wizards of Rolan, I assure you if anything happens to him, they'll all be out for blood."

"Let's put assassination off the table," the guild master said. "As Grandmother rightly points out, wizards owe him and the emperor a great deal."

"If you don't want to kill him then what?" Tal asked. "Reasoning has clearly failed."

"There is magic that can alter a person's thoughts," Esmay of Lasil said. "While I have no doubt that he is strong willed, if we could work on him over a period of time, I'm sure between us we could wear down whatever resistance he might possess. When the job was finished, we'd have a willing ally instead of a corpse or an enemy."

"I second Esmay's plan," Cypher said. If they could make it work, it would eliminate the problem without starting a war they couldn't win.

"Are there any objections?" the guild master asked.

Tal looked like he wanted to smash something, but he held his tongue as did everyone else.

"Very well. We will attempt Esmay's suggestion. Capturing Otto will be the biggest challenge. A large enough group could certainly suppress his magic but getting him to show up will be the challenge. Certainly, if any of us suggest it, he will be on guard and likely not alone."

"He did express willingness to consider a meeting and I

know someone who might be willing to help nudge him to commit," Cypher said. "Enoch is Otto's teacher and a former member of the underground. His help might be enough."

The guild master's cowled head bobbed. "I leave it to you then, Cypher. A team will be ready as soon as you have a time and place for the meeting. This meeting is ended."

The other guild leaders headed for the exit. Cypher brought up the rear, his mind busy. Convincing Enoch to lead his prize pupil into a trap wasn't going to be easy, but somehow he'd do it. The alternative didn't bear thinking about.

～

Otto watched as Corina wove a pair of threads together then ran lightning through them. Sparks flew but did no damage. They were practicing in the yard outside the portal fort. Her skills had improved since he last saw her. She could now cast Lightning Bolt in under two seconds. Still too slow for a real fight, but far better than when he first showed her the spell.

When she finally let the threads vanish and with them the sparks, all the guards that had been watching clapped in appreciation. Portal duty was boring and the men no doubt appreciated a bit of entertainment.

Corina bowed then smiled at Otto. "How was that?"

"Much better. I think it's time you learned a new spell."

Her eyes gleamed in anticipation. "Which one?"

"Resonant Binding." Otto dug the gift he'd made for her out of his pocket. The simple iron ring was smooth and polished on the outside and marked with runes on the inside.

The markings wouldn't affect her magic, but would allow him to track her should she get into trouble. Much as he hated to invest too much in any one person, he had high hopes for Corina. And on top of that he just liked talking to the girl. All she wanted was to learn magic, unlike many of the other people he had to deal with every day.

She held the ring in one hand and ran a finger over it. "This is for me?"

"Yes. You can't use this spell without an iron ring. Try it on. I had to guess the size, but if it doesn't fit, alterations are simple enough."

Corina tried her right ring finger, scowled, and moved on to the middle finger. She brightened. "That'll work. What now?"

"Now..." Otto looked around for a test subject. Oskar had the bad luck to emerge from the fort just as he did. "Oskar! Come here a moment."

The spy hurried over. "Lord Shenk, how may I be of service?"

"Corina needs a test target. You just volunteered."

Oskar blanched, no doubt thinking about their last test subject, the late king of Rolan.

"Relax, this spell is both harmless and painless. You'll be fine." Otto turned to Corina. "Okay, send a thread of ether through the iron ring then out into Oskar. When the thread touches Oskar, you should sense a vibration. Focus on that. You need to spread the ether into everything that vibrates."

Her face scrunched up as she concentrated. The ether flowed through her ring and out into Oskar. "Like that?"

"Oskar, can you move?" Otto asked.

Oskar lifted both arms then stopped. "My legs are frozen, but everything above the waist is still under my control."

"You didn't get everything," Otto said. "Hone your focus and find the vibrations you missed."

They went on like that until she'd fully bound Oskar and was drenched in sweat.

"Wow, that's hard," Corina said.

"You can release the spell." When she had, Otto turned to Oskar. "You're good, thanks for the help."

He bowed. "Always a pleasure to serve, Lord Shenk." The spy hurried off before Otto could think of something else for him to do.

"Don't worry, Corina, that's one of the simplest resonance spells. You just need practice. Your best bet is to find a dog or something to cast the spell on every day. You need to be able to use it quickly, like the lightning."

She brushed sweat-soaked hair out of her eyes. "Are all the spells going to be this hard at first?"

"No, most will be harder. These are the simplest kinds of magic. You need to build up your mental and physical stamina. That takes years, not weeks or months. I trained with a single thread for over a decade before even attempting a second. If you keep at it, you'll get there." Otto glanced at the shadows. Much as he preferred to stay here and play at magic, he needed to get back. Hopefully Allen had found them a useable property. "You keep practicing. I need to go."

"Already? You've only been here for a couple days."

Otto smiled. It was nice to have at least one person, besides Wolfric, that enjoyed his company and wasn't afraid of him. "I know, but the empire is still unsettled. Eventually I'll be able to take more time to enjoy myself, but not now. See you later."

He became one with the ether and quickly traveled to Franken Manor. From his bedroom, it was a short walk to his office. Otto strode through the door and frowned when he saw a note sitting on his desk. He didn't like anyone coming in here, even the servants. Not that he kept anything secret or incriminating anywhere so obvious, he just didn't like people messing with his stuff. Hopefully it wasn't a new problem. He had plenty of things do already.

Things seemed to be calm in Rolan, for the moment anyway. In the capital, people were out and about, kids played in the streets, and five merchants had traveled through the portal that morning to trade in Garenland. That was the most since the war ended. Oskar had informed him, the day before he became a practice dummy, that there had been no raids and next to no bandit activity. All in all, matters were as good as he dared to hope. That Corina was improving was a nice bonus.

Otto snatched the note off his desk. Master Enoch wanted to speak with him as soon as he returned. What could the old man want? Maybe he was bored and looking for a new assignment. Otto could probably find him something, they could always use more wizards to help rebuild Marduke.

He shrugged, tossed the note away, and went outside. Enoch was waiting in the barracks they'd built for wizard trainees. It was kind of sad, seeing him sitting alone at the long table.

"You wanted to see me, Master?" Otto asked.

"Lord Shenk, thank you for coming. Cypher reached out to me again. He wondered if you had forgotten about your offer to speak with the guild master. I volunteered to pass along the message."

Otto hadn't forgotten, he just didn't think there was much point. "I've made my position clear. I don't think there's anything more to discuss."

"Maybe she has a new proposal, something that would work for both of you. Please, my lord. I would consider it a personal favor if you would hear her out."

Otto figured it was more likely a trap than an honest meeting. But on the off chance it wasn't, maybe a short chat with the person actually in charge would be worthwhile.

"I'll consider it. I suppose I'll need to speak with Cypher to arrange the details?"

"That was his request. And thank you for considering it. The underground helped a lot of wizards. If you can make some sort of peace with them, it would be good for everyone."

Otto would make peace with them alright. Whether they were dead or alive to enjoy it was another matter altogether.

CHAPTER 23

U ther was relieved to see Markane's harbor in the distance. The trip had been smooth and calm, but still, he'd be glad to get off this bloody ship. He was very much a creature of the mountains and forests. Being stuck in a space sixty paces long was making him stir-crazy.

He took a deep breath of the salty air and tried to focus. When he met with Valtan he couldn't show any weakness. The fact that he'd been driven from his home and rescued by Markane agents was bad enough. Damned if he was going to give anyone any other reasons to think he was weak.

The ship sailed between a pair of towers into the harbor. Uther looked up and saw ballistae and catapults ready to rain death down on anyone that didn't belong. Even without Valtan's magic, trying to take the city would be nearly impossible, at least from the ocean side.

A couple dozen ships of all sizes were tied up in the harbor. The captain guided them with an expert hand to one of the farthest-out berths. Ropes were tossed and tied off in intricate knots. The whole process took about ten minutes then the gangplank was lowered.

Uther couldn't get down it fast enough.

Waiting for him was King Eddred, the so-called ruler of Markane. Of course, everyone knew the truth. He was little more than a puppet for the Arcane Lord as had been all of his ancestors for centuries. Seeing as how he was the only king still nominally in charge of his country, rather than dead or a Garenland lackey, maybe he'd made a wise choice after all.

Eddred offered a polite nod. "Uther, welcome to Markane."

"Thank you. I appreciate your hospitality." Uther nearly choked on his gratitude, but he wasn't such a savage that he'd ignore what had been done to help him. "How fares the war against Garenland?"

Eddred's smile held no humor. "There is no war, not really. Villares is dead, Liatos a prisoner in Garen, and Philippa and Kasimir both agreed to become governors. You were our best hope, but that didn't work out. I'm sure Lord Valtan will think of some other plan. Come on, I'll show you to the palace."

Uther's mind reeled as he walked along beside Eddred. Could there truly be no active resistance to Garenland's rule? He couldn't believe it.

"When did Villares fall?" Uther asked. "Last I heard he still had a large force under his command and was fighting a running battle with the enemy."

"A couple weeks ago I believe. Garenland forced him into a decisive battle. Our spies say they burned every village they came to, turning the people out to live in the wild. The Garenlanders swore they'd keep burning until Villares surrendered. He couldn't of course, too proud, but he did go down fighting. He even took a few of the enemy with him for all the good it did."

Uther doubted Eddred knew much about a warrior's pride. Not that he was in any position to criticize, having fled rather than die with his men. He envied Villares his end.

They reached the palace without incident and Eddred guided him through tapestry-lined halls to a war room where Valtan waited.

The Arcane Lord turned his almost-electric gaze on Uther. "Congratulations on your survival. What happened?"

"The weapons you provided were destroyed by a Garenland patrol and the Lady in Red gave up the location of our meeting place, curse her spineless soul. We marched into a trap and only I escaped. If not for your ship, I'd likely be dead or chained in the mines with my father right now."

"The alchemical weapons didn't give you a big enough advantage?" Valtan asked.

"They worked wonderfully for the first minute or so, then the cursed wizards figured out that they could redirect the exploding jars, often right back into the face of the man throwing it." Uther shrugged. He couldn't very well get angry with Valtan. The weapons worked fine; they just couldn't replace a wizard.

"Given the haste with which they were trained, I had hoped they only knew basic attack and defense spells. If they can do telekinesis as well, hand-thrown weapons will be useless." Valtan nodded, more to himself it seemed than to Uther. "Thank you. When it comes time to counterattack, that information will be invaluable."

"I'm glad I could offer something of value for my life. I—"

The war room door burst open and a soldier staggered in gasping for air. "The... Garenlanders."

"What about them?" Valtan demanded.

"They're here. On West Barrier Island." The soldier

straightened but couldn't meet Valtan's gaze. "They've burned two villages at least. A survivor arrived only moments ago."

"They dare attack Markane directly!?" Valtan roared. "Of all the stupid, arrogant acts. I will see their nation burned to ash for this insult."

"Will you counterattack with your magic?" Uther asked.

When the furious gaze turned on him, he wished he'd kept quiet. But instead of striking him down Valtan seemed to regain his composure. "I can't. My magic doesn't reach beyond the main island and I can't leave the city. Somehow they know it. That's why the attacks are on the barrier islands."

"Otto Shenk must have sent them," Eddred said. "That young man is entirely too sharp for our own good."

"He's the one you mentioned before, that spoke to you in Lux and warned us not to interfere?" Valtan asked.

"Yes, and he was here at the conclave," Eddred said. "You must remember him. Otto was the only other wizard."

"I vaguely remember a piddling excuse for a wizard that day, but I hardly took note of him. Perhaps I should have. If he was perceptive enough to understand my limitations that argues for more training than anyone living could provide." Valtan stroked his chin and made a circle around the map table. "Dispatch two ships loaded with soldiers. They can't have a very large force. Once we've dealt with them, I will consider how best to repay Otto Shenk for this insult."

"Can I be of some help?" Uther asked.

"Not at the moment," Valtan said. "You've had a long, difficult journey. Rest, recover. When the time is right, you'll get your chance."

Stephan tore a strip of meat from a joint of roasted pork and sighed as the savory juice filled his mouth. It had been far too long since he'd enjoyed fresh pork. The last boar hunt he went on came up empty then he had to listen to Griswalda complain that he'd been gone for three days. The only reason he hadn't strangled the woman was that her father was still alive and ruled the next county over.

The last thing Shenk Barony needed was a fight with them. They'd win it of course, but the losses would be a waste and Father hated wasting what he might otherwise own. The old man was still strong enough and had the loyalty of enough men that Stephan didn't dare kill him either. Soon enough he'd end them both, but not yet.

A scream in the distance brought a smile to his face. Sounded like the men were enjoying the spoils of their third village. The loot had been pathetic, but the girls were pretty enough. Shame they had to kill them before moving on, but he couldn't have a line of prisoners slowing him down. It was only a matter of time before someone showed up and he wanted to be ready.

Jost appeared out of the evening gloom and strode up to Stephan's fire. "Lord Shenk. I've completed the inventory. I'd value the spoils at a little over five hundred golden eagles."

Stephan spat out a piece of gristle. "Pathetic. If I wasn't having so much fun, this expedition would be a complete waste of time."

"It is nice fighting these weaklings. I haven't lost a man yet. Even if the pay isn't great, making it through unharmed is a nice bonus."

"Don't count on that lasting. Even Markane will muster a defense eventually."

Jost raised a mug of stolen wine. "Then we should enjoy ourselves while we can."

A flash like lightning filled the air and Otto appeared. Dressed all in black, he looked like a demon, at least until you saw his youthful face. Stephan had a hard time believing his baby brother had really done all the things they claimed. Then again, he remembered the look on Otto's face when he found Stephan with his lovely wife. That face could have committed horrors.

"How do you fare?" Otto asked. "You appear to be having an easy time of it."

"I'll leave you to your discussion." Jost hurried away into the night, the coward.

"So far we have," Stephan said. He refused to show any fear to his brother despite the nervous flutter in his gut. "Join me for dinner?"

"I have already eaten. I only wanted to warn you that Prince Uther escaped Axel and is, I believe, headed to Markane. I doubt he'll leave the capital, but if you should by some chance encounter him, his head will bring you a nice bonus, say, one hundred double eagles."

Stephan grinned. "So now I need to clean up Axel's mess. Wouldn't be the first time. Maybe this prince can put up a decent fight. No one else on this miserable island can."

"Don't underestimate Uther. He evaded capture for months and even did a little damage. It was impressive considering his limited resources. Anyway, that's all I wanted to tell you. I'll check in again in a week or so."

As quickly as he appeared, Otto vanished. A shiver ran up Stephan's spine. The days of anyone, him included, bullying Otto were long gone. And should anyone think otherwise, heaven help them.

CHAPTER 24

Otto had barely become one with the ether and left his brother behind when a powerful force dragged him off his intended course. He tried to fight it, but he would have had a better chance of fighting a bear off with a toothpick.

When the movement finally stopped, he found himself facing another person, their ethereal body glowing like the sun. It could only be Lord Valtan. Otto didn't think he'd gotten close enough for him to reach out like this. Actually Otto didn't know someone could grab his ethereal body at all.

"Calm yourself." Valtan's voice sounded exactly as Otto remembered from their previous meeting. "We cannot harm each other here."

"Then what do you want?" Otto asked.

"To understand. Why have you chosen this path? If you are here, then you have already overcome the first of your natural limitations. You and I may well be the only two living beings able to come to this place. It is only natural that I wished to greet you properly."

"You didn't think much of me the first time we met. When you looked at me with such disdain, I swore to myself that one day we would stand face to face again and you would acknowledge me as your equal. That day is not today, but I will get there."

Valtan shook his head. "You wish to become an Arcane Lord? Don't. It isn't worth giving up your humanity."

"What are you talking about? You seemed as human as any other man I've met."

"My outer form may appear human, but it is only an appearance. I assume you found a book or scroll my former apprentice left lying about that taught you how to break through the first barrier, did it not explain what doing so meant?"

Otto doubted mentioning that he'd spoken directly to Lord Karonin's spirit would be wise. "No, it only said that if I wished to grow stronger, I had to find a way through the pain. I did, excruciating though it was. I've grown stronger than I ever dreamed possible. What more do I need to know?"

"You need to know why it hurt so much. The pain is a warning. What you've done is replace most of your soul with pure ether. Surely you've noticed some changes. The Bliss now comes less readily and only when you perform especially powerful magic. Your emotions have grown stunted. Things that once would have turned your stomach now barely elicit a passing thought. Love and hate, fear and joy, none of them move you the way they used to. This change is what led my former comrades to commit acts of carnage in the quest for power that no sane human would."

Otto couldn't deny that hurting others had become far easier. He'd assumed it was a result of all the pain he'd suffered, but maybe the magic had changed him. Then again, maybe

Valtan was trying to scare him off before he could become a true rival.

"You mentioned a first barrier. That implies that there's at least a second."

"Yes, the first is the limit of the mortal soul, the second is the limit of mortal flesh. At a certain point your body simply can't control the amount of ether you want to use and keep its physical form. The magic will literally blow you apart. The pain before you reach that will make your earlier efforts seem like a tickle. You've reached that point, haven't you?"

"I'm close," Otto admitted. "That's why I need to make the transformation. Until I become like you, I'll never reach my full potential."

"Perhaps not as a wizard, but you can as a person. To become like me is to give up everything that makes you human. Your emotions will be gone. No atrocity will be too horrible to consider. You'll never feel a connection to another person. I would give all the power I've gained to get that back. It's not too late for you. Though you'll remain emotionally stunted, you can still find pleasure in life. Take it from me, the trade isn't worth it."

He sounded sincere, but Otto had learned the hard way that faking sincerity wasn't that difficult. Annamaria had taught him that.

"I'll take your words under consideration. Please take mine to heart as well. I seek no war, neither with you nor anyone else. Leave the portals in my care and I will use them only on the old schedule. I will recall my raiders before they can do any more harm to your people. I only wish to study and learn more about magic. What do you say?"

Valtan shook his head. "I can't. The more you learn the more potential harm you could do with the portals. Return control to me and I will reinstate the Portal Compact with Garenland as a full member. We'll eliminate the rule that got you kicked out so no one else can exploit it."

"You want me to give up everything we've gained and return to the old system? No, too many of our people have died. I can't do it and even if I wanted to, Emperor Wolfric would never agree."

"Then it seems we must remain enemies. If I see you in person, I will show no mercy."

Otto nodded. "Nor will I show any to you."

The same force that grabbed Otto now hurled him away. He quickly regained control and willed himself back home. Stephan wasn't going to be enough to dissuade Markane. Having spoken directly to Valtan, Otto understood what he was facing.

Extreme measures would be necessary.

Valtan appeared in his meditation chamber. The austere room held only a thick rug where he sat to gather his thoughts. He had barely sensed the young wizard passing through the ether, but when he did, he knew he had to try and convince him to follow a different path. After their conversation, he felt little confidence that he had succeeded. He had sensed no lies from the boy, but he still couldn't allow him to retain control of the portals. If he ever truly learned what they were capable of...

He shuddered. Best to hope that never happened. When he took a step toward the door, Valtan wobbled and had to catch himself. The constant drain from the portals' random activation had left him weaker than he liked to believe. There was a part of him that was tempted to accept Otto's offer of a truce and to hell with the risks. But the portals were his responsibility and he couldn't shirk that. It just pained him to see another wizard committing the same folly that he and the others did so long ago. That he was the only one that had ever seen it that way was a tragedy in his eyes.

Though Valtan had said he would defeat Otto and his armies, the truth was he had limited resources with which to do that. Markane had never been especially populous and the idea of them invading even a small country was laughable. On top of that, their few wizards weren't trained to fight, only protect.

It was a necessary precaution. The last thing he wanted was another Otto Shenk rising up right under his nose.

CHAPTER 25

Captain Wainwright stood at the helm of his ship and eased the wheel around. He'd been patrolling the area around West Barrier Island for over a week while the raiders did their thing. He was happy to be rid of them truth be told. Their leader, Stephan, was as obnoxious a man as he'd ever met, even for a noble. His brother, the wizard, had been cool but polite and thoughtful when approaching him with an offer of work.

The job was easy enough anyway. Land the raiders, patrol the area around the island, and pick them up when they'd collected all the loot they could. The pay was potentially good, and the risks minimal.

"Sail on the western horizon!" the lookout called.

Why didn't he listen to his mother? Never tempt fate.

"Make that two sails!"

He glanced heavenward and shook his head. "I didn't mean to complain, I swear."

No chorus of angels appeared to tell him everything would be okay. "Helmsman, take the wheel."

Wainwright hurried to the bow, digging his spyglass out as he went. Sure enough, the ships were flying the Markane flag. Figures were climbing the rigging and on deck soldiers waited. This had to be their response to the raiders. At least neither ship had a catapult.

"Wizards on deck!" Wainwright bellowed. "Signal our sister ship and tell them to prepare for battle!"

The flag man started waving while he went to meet a pair of skinny kids barely over twenty who emerged from below deck. The boy and girl both had long hair and wore black and gold uniforms. The two wizards—they hadn't actually been introduced to him—rubbed their silver rings.

"What's the trouble, Captain?" the boy asked.

"Enemy ship. Dealing with them is your task I believe."

"It is indeed. May I borrow your spyglass?" The boy held out his hand and Wainwright set the precious item in it.

"Isn't this exciting?" The girl looked even younger when she smiled.

Though it was none of his business Wainwright asked, "How old are you, miss?"

"Eighteen. When Lord Shenk gave me this assignment and my ring he looked right at me and said I had great potential. Me. A complete nobody from a town so small it doesn't even have a name. No one has ever treated me with that kind of respect, certainly no one as important as him. I have to do a good job. Prove I'm worthy of the trust he's put in me."

"I have a ring too you know." The boy lowered the spyglass. "They're too far away to make out any details. We need to get closer to attack."

"How close?" Wainwright asked.

"A hundred yards or so."

The girl nodded her agreement.

Wainwright scratched his chin and studied the sky. "We'll have the wind advantage on the first pass; you'll have to make it count."

"We won't need a second," the girl said.

The boy scowled at her. "Remember what Master Enoch said, don't get overconfident. They might have wizards too."

"Bet they aren't as strong as us," she countered.

"If you aim for the sails," Wainwright said, hoping to forestall an argument. "It won't matter what happens after that. If they can't maneuver, we'll wipe them out."

He left the youthful wizards and returned to his place at the wheel. A half turn sent them directly at the first enemy vessel. Their companion ship changed course to join them. He sent a silent prayer up that the kids were as talented as they thought they were.

Yard by yard the four ships closed. Every second Wainwright expected some magical attack to come roaring at him.

But none ever did. When they had nearly reached the target distance, a glow formed on deck. Orange flames danced around the wizards' outstretched hands. A moment later two fireballs arced out toward the enemy ships. The attacks stayed high, aiming for their sails.

Both spells shattered against an invisible barrier. Just as the boy thought, the enemy had a wizard as well.

Wainwright braced himself for a counterattack, but one never came.

His wizards put their heads together.

The enemy ship was nearly past.

Further to the left, the second Markane ship was ablaze, its sails burning like tinder.

He shifted his attention to the wizards and found them glowing again. This time a single fireball went toward the sails.

A moment before it reached the barrier, the girl fired a lightning bolt at the ship's waterline.

The fireball splashed against the shield, but the lightning bolt struck home, blowing a three-foot hole in their hull. Water rushed in and they began to list at once.

Wainwright turned the wheel to put some distance between them. The wizards ran up to join him. Both looked weary, but proud.

"Good job, you two," he said.

They smiled and the girl said, "They only had one wizard and he could only protect half the ship."

"Saving the sails does little good if your ship sinks," the boy added.

Wainwright couldn't argue with that. He guided the ship a comfortable distance away and watched for enemy longboats. It wouldn't do much good to sink the big ship only to let the little ones continue on their way.

The only thing he knew for sure was that he was glad he didn't have to fight enemy wizards. They were in a new world. A dangerous one.

CHAPTER 26

After his unsettling visit with Valtan in the ether, Otto was relieved to get back and more concerned than ever about the future of the empire. While he had no doubt Stephan was doing his best to slaughter every islander he could find, Otto now understood that wouldn't be enough to dissuade Markane. Valtan appeared hell bent on recovering control of the portals.

Why was another matter. Otto doubted his activating them off schedule was more than an inconvenience to the Arcane Lord. There had to be something he was missing. Maybe Lord Karonin would have some insight. He hadn't visited his master in months. He meant to, it was just that things kept coming up. That, unfortunately, didn't seem likely to change anytime soon.

Otto finished washing up, put on fresh clothes, and strode out of his room. It was late evening and he was eager to find out if Allen had found a new base for them.

He had barely taken a step down the staircase when the clatter of utensils on porcelain informed him that he'd taken the wrong route. The gurgly laugh of a baby confirmed his fear. The family, it seemed, had gathered for dinner.

Before Otto could retreat, Edwyn called out, "Otto, my boy. I didn't realize you were in or I'd have sent someone to fetch you for dinner. Come join us, we've only just begun."

Eating with the in-laws was the last thing Otto wanted to do right now, but he was hungry and the food was always delicious. Besides, it would be good for Edwyn to see him and Annamaria together. The time was fast approaching when he wouldn't have to pretend anymore, but for now things remained too fragile to rock the boat.

Otto made his way to the dining room. As always, the table was laden with a dozen platters of food. Edwyn sat at the head in his billowing white robes with Annamaria to his left. Otto refused to focus on her. Somehow, she remained as beautiful as the first time he laid eyes on her. Two seats down Mimi held Abby and fed her some mushed-up pale glop. Otto took the seat to Edwyn's right.

"Good evening," Otto said. "You seem in fine spirits tonight."

Annamaria refused to meet his gaze, but Edwyn beamed. "Absolutely. Trade has finally begun to recover. We're doing excellent business in Lasil and Lux. Even Rolan's market has perked up. Profits are coming in and not just ours, the other merchants are smiling as well. There is one thing..."

"The portal auctions?" Otto helped himself to a salmon steak, buttered leeks, and a slice of bread.

"Exactly. I did understand correctly that we would retain the rights, didn't I?"

Otto swallowed a sigh. He'd been dreading this conversation even though he knew it had to happen eventually.

"Matters have changed. Given the necessary security

precautions, the portal guard will be handling access and fee collections. Since we now control all the portals, the change, while unfortunate, is necessary. You understand, I hope?"

"Yes, yes, never fear." Edwyn tried to sound upbeat and failed miserably. No doubt he anticipated collecting a percentage from six portals instead of just one. With the cost of maintaining the portal guard, they simply couldn't afford to pay a pointless cut.

Otto ate quickly and excused himself. No one objected to his quick departure. Passing through the gates of Gold Ward at night was sometimes a bother, but by now all the guards knew him and knew better than to cause any delay.

The business district after dark could be sketchy, especially the area near Allen's tavern. Otto would have welcomed a robbery attempt. Killing a few hapless thugs would be a good way to vent his frustration. Damaging Annamaria's pretty face would have been more satisfying, but as an old friend of Wolfric's, he didn't dare let anything happen to her. Too many questions down that path.

The Thirsty Sprite had a fair crowd when Otto arrived. Light and laughter spilled out the door when he pushed it open. He didn't resent others their happiness. In fact, he regarded it as a sign that the new empire was thriving.

Behind the bar Allen was busy filling tankards while his collection of cute barmaids hustled around making deliveries. There was no sign of Ulf or Sin which he assumed meant they were at the new base.

Allen spotted him as he got closer and nodded toward the far end of the bar away from the bulk of the guests. "Lord Shenk. I found a place. A warehouse six blocks from here. The owner died and his heirs were keen to sell. Ulf and Sin are getting their respective endeavors set up as we speak. It was such a good deal I didn't dare wait for you to approve before I made the purchase. I need to pay off the contract in five days."

"Get me the details and I'll arrange the money tomorrow. I trust all has been quiet while I was away?"

"As far as I know. My contacts haven't mentioned anything and Sin hasn't brought any issues to my attention. Even the Wizards Guild has been quiet."

Otto nodded, pleased that Cypher hadn't made any further attempts to hire muscle. It seemed for the moment they were taking his threats to heart. That was good since he meant every word. Maybe he would humor his mentor and take a meeting with the guild master. There had to be some course of action that would satisfy everyone.

"I can see you're busy. Get me those purchase details and tell me how to find the warehouse and I'll get out of your hair."

Five minutes later Otto was on the move again. The contract was rolled up in his satchel unread. Unless the price was totally unreasonable, he'd simply pay it. It wasn't like he was lacking in resources. The only reason he planned to use Franken money rather than Crown coin was to avoid drawing attention. They were supposed to be a semi-secret organization after all.

The warehouse was easy enough to find. The huge double doors in the front were emblazoned with a shield crossed with two swords. Apparently, the previous owner made weapons and armor. No surprise given that before the war, those were Garenland's biggest exports. Now, of course, weapon sales were banned since they had no desire to sell high-quality gear to people who might want to kill them down the road.

To the right of the main doors was a smaller door for easier access. Light shone through the crack at the bottom. Toward the rear of the vast empty space, a group of men were busy setting up tables and putting heavy glass containers on them, all under Ulf's watchful eyes. On the left, Sin was talking with two people, a man and a woman from their builds.

Sin could conduct her business without him looking over her shoulder. He went to check on Ulf. "Do you have everything you need?"

Ulf jumped, clearly having no idea Otto had entered. "Yes, I'll be ready to begin working tomorrow. Which reminds me. Other than the drug, do you have anything else you'd like me to make?"

Otto scratched his chin and discovered he'd need to shave when he got home. "I'm not certain. What else can you make?"

"Well, I can make exploding jars like those used against your troops in Straken. Knockout drugs if you want to capture someone. There's always the hangover cure and some other simple remedies common in the Celestial Empire that I haven't seen here."

"Make some of everything except the exploding jars. Should it be necessary, the wizards will handle that kind of thing. The simple things might make a good source of funds for our work. The less attention we draw within the government the better. We'll have to set up a front company, but that's a simple matter. A legitimate business would explain the warehouse as well."

Otto nodded to himself. Things were shaping up nicely. If he could settle things with the Wizards Guild, he'd feel pretty good about the state of the empire.

○

First thing the next morning, Otto made his way to the palace. He hadn't spoken to Wolfric in far too long. Not that he was avoiding the new emperor, but other matters had kept him busy. Otto hoped to catch him at breakfast before court soured his mood.

After being waved through by the guards, Otto made his way to the emperor's bedchamber. Apparently Wolfric was dining in comfort this morning. The two palace guards snapped to attention when he approached and the one on the right rapped twice on the door before announcing, "Otto Shenk, Majesty."

"Send him in."

The guard opened the door and Otto stepped through. Thankfully Wolfric was dressed, albeit in a simple tunic and trousers rather than his official robes of state. He sat at a small table laden with all his favorites.

Wolfric waved him into the seat opposite and said, "I don't know what all you've been doing, my friend, but the merchants are happy and even the nobles have kept their complaints to a minimum. Will you join me?"

Otto fixed himself something to eat then said, "You received my report about Villares?"

"Yes, good riddance. I've dispatched a new governor and ordered the Southern Legion deployed throughout the country. That should keep things calm. General Varchi wrote and said whatever you did at the mines, they haven't had a riot in a week."

Otto smiled. He'd have to remember to thank Ulf. "I spoke with Lord Valtan yesterday."

Wolfric's eyes nearly bugged out of his head. "How? Why?"

"I assure you it wasn't my idea. After I checked in with

Stephan and started home Valtan grabbed me and yanked me into a conversation in the ether. Basically he said nothing short of returning control of all the portals to him would be enough to stop Markane from fighting us."

"Should we recall your brother?" Wolfric asked.

"No, he'll at least give them something to think about. Besides, Stephan seems to be having a grand time. Having met his wife, I can't begrudge him a bit of fun. I'm working on a more aggressive response, but I'll need a day or two to get everything ready."

"And the Wizards Guild?"

Otto made a face and took a bite of his toast. "That's another thing I need to straighten out. The guild master wants to meet me face to face. I assume they're planning an ambush of some sort, but if there's any chance of making an arrangement, I can't ignore them."

Wolfric gave a rueful shake of his head. "And here I've been complaining about boredom. I want you to know that the empire in general and me in particular are very grateful for everything you're doing. Don't forget, if you ever need anything, just ask. If it's within my power to grant your wish, I'll happily do so."

"I appreciate that, my friend, I truly do. Now let's eat up. I have an errand to run."

CHAPTER 27

Otto appeared in the magical armory and agitated the ether. He smiled as he looked around at all the wonderful magic. He needed to become an Arcane Lord just to have time enough to study everything collected here. Tempting as it was to while away a few hours in the library, Otto forced his gaze away from the hundreds of tomes his master had collected over her long life and walked over to the artifact table.

The only item he'd taken was a single box of mithril rings. Today he was after something more sinister. He couldn't remember which visit he'd noticed the shiny black box, but he did remember opening it and reading the note inside. Dangerous, to be used in the most extreme circumstances only. Well, circumstances were pretty extreme when you had an immortal wizard determined to see you defeated.

He found the box where he'd left it, at the very edge of the table. Otto ran a finger along the cool, smooth surface. The box felt like it was made from polished black stone rather than wood. And maybe it was for all he knew. What mattered now was what was inside.

A small, white skull stared at him from inside the box. Beside it was a matching bone-white ring. The skull was a death magic item created by Lord Amet Sur, the mightiest Arcane Lord of them all. When dropped into a water supply, the skull would dissolve and spread a magical plague. If you touched the skull with your bare hand and weren't wearing the ring, death was instantaneous. Of course a wizard could get around that by wrapping the skull in a bubble of ether.

Maybe Valtan was right and the magic was turning him into some kind of emotionless monster. Would he have been able to even consider something like this before breaking through his personal barrier? Perhaps, but he doubted it.

He pulled his hand away from the open box, snarled at himself, slapped it shut, and slipped it into his satchel. Otto was going to win this bloody war and if it cost him his soul then so be it.

The box felt like a lead weight as he walked to a different table, this one on the opposite side of the chamber from the library. Otto had never paid much heed to the wealth sitting there just waiting to be taken, but today it would come in handy. He grabbed a small pouch filled with gold nuggets and added that to his collection. That much gold could set a man up for life. Hopefully it could also bribe someone to risk his life.

Otto let the ether calm and darkness returned to the armory. He took a deep breath and become one with the ether. He doubted Valtan would want to have another chat, but you never knew. Even knowing the Arcane Lord couldn't harm him in the ether did little to reduce his anxiety as he raced toward Stephan.

Fortunately, Otto reached his brother without incident. He appeared in the center of a burning village. Stephan stood watching his troops running down the survivors and dragging the women to a holding area where half a dozen soldiers watched over them.

Stephan raised an eyebrow when he finally noticed Otto. "I didn't expect to see you again so soon."

"Likewise. Unfortunately, I need to take more aggressive measures to convince Valtan to end the conflict."

"Are you recalling us?"

"Not at all. You can slaughter everyone on the barrier islands if you want. But it has been made clear to me that won't stop him. I need to strike at the capital."

Stephan's laugh was nearly drowned out by someone screaming in the village. "You said we couldn't go near the capital and now you want me to march my men to their deaths?"

"No, I need one volunteer to deliver a magical weapon." Otto pulled out the pouch of gold and opened it. "The reward will be considerable."

Stephan looked at the gold as though considering delivering the weapon himself. "Won't Valtan sense a magical weapon approaching?"

"No, at least not this one. The magic only activates under specific circumstances. Otherwise it appears as a harmless bauble. A creepy harmless bauble, but still nothing anyone would give a second look. Think any of your men has the guts?"

Stephan shrugged. The sounds of fighting had died down. He loosed a piercing whistle that brought soldiers running from every direction. When all but those guarding the women had arrived, he laid out Otto's proposal.

"So, who wants to earn a pouch of gold?" Stephan asked at last.

The mercenaries all looked at each other but no one spoke up. Finally, one of the garrison soldiers said, "I'll do it, my lord."

"Good man." Stephan clapped him on the shoulder.

"What do I have to do?" the soldier asked.

Otto took out the black box, opened it, removed the ring, and handed it over. "Put that on. It will protect you from the magic. The task is simple. Infiltrate the capital, find a public well, and drop the skull into it. The magic will activate automatically. As soon as you've done that, leave. Rejoin your comrades and collect your reward. I'll take the ring back when we see each other again."

"That's all?" the soldier asked.

Otto nodded. "Just be certain you don't take off the ring. There are bound to be groups of people fleeing toward the capital, you should have no trouble mingling with them."

They waited while he stripped off his armor and weapons. When he was finally ready, Otto held out the box and he took the skull.

"Good luck," Otto said.

With the infiltrator had left and the others resumed looting, Stephan asked, "What does that weapon do exactly?"

"It kills cities."

○

Uther had so far spent most of his time in Markane studying in the war room. Not that there was a ton to study. Garenland had fairly thoroughly crushed everything that might resist them. Uther included himself in that. Proud as he was, there was no denying that he had failed miserably to dislodge Straken's ancient enemies from his home.

Restoring the continent was going to be even harder since they had no foothold. Landing troops by ship might work, but they still needed to find soldiers. Markane certainly wasn't going to provide them. Maybe if he could reach out to those that resented Garenland, Uther could convince them to join the fight.

He looked down at the map, trying in vain to think of a likely place to begin. His musing was cut short when the door burst open and one of the palace messengers entered. "My lord, His Majesty requests you come to the throne room at once."

"What's happened?"

"A ship has returned. Please."

Uther nodded and fell in behind the messenger. A ship had returned? It could only be one of the two ship they'd dispatched to ferry troops to the barrier island. No way should they be back already. Something must have gone wrong.

When they reached the throne room, Eddred and Valtan were standing beside the throne. They had been joined by a dirty, soot-stained man in a sailor's uniform.

Eddred waved Uther up beside them. "I thought you'd want to hear this."

Uther appreciated the gesture. Even though he was only a guest with no rights here, everyone had gone out of their way to include him in their planning.

"Go ahead," Valtan said.

"My lords, our mission failed. My ship suffered the loss of all sails and our sister vessel was sunk. The enemy had wizards, strong ones. They blasted through our hull with minimal effort. I didn't expect such powerful opponents to be assigned to a raider ship."

Valtan scowled. "How many threads did they wield?"

"Seventeen between them, but the threads were thick, denser than any magic I've seen, other than yours of course. I just don't understand how they could be so much stronger than us."

"It would seem Otto Shenk has learned the secret of mithril," Valtan muttered, more to himself than the others.

Uther didn't know what any of it meant beyond the mission had failed. "Let me take some soldiers and hunt them down. We'll go over land, across the bridge. It will take longer, but we won't have to deal with enemy ships."

Everyone looked at him and Uther had a moment of self-consciousness. This wasn't his country. Maybe he should have kept his mouth shut. But he was committed now. "This is what I'm good at. I led the rangers back home for years. Father thought I was of more worth in the wilds than I was at court. It was something we both agreed on wholeheartedly."

"I have no objection," Eddred said, looking to Valtan.

"Very well. The invaders need to be dealt with. But take no risks. You are of considerable value to us."

Uther didn't know how much time Valtan had spent out in the field, but every moment you were beyond the city walls was a risk. Playing it safe accomplished little.

If he died, at least he could take a few of the enemy down with him.

ᔆ

W hen Uther had left to collect his weapon and armor, Eddred said, "I should go and ready a force for him. We'll be pushing things pretty thin in the capital. How many do you think I should send?"

Valtan didn't appear to have heard him. The wizard was staring off into space, likely at something Eddred couldn't even perceive. He was used to it and waited patiently until Valtan's eyes refocused.

He asked his question again and this time Valtan replied. "The capital is in no danger as long as I'm here. Uther needs enough people to get the job done and given our soldiers' lack of combat experience, I'd say you need to send at least five hundred."

Eddred winced. That was nearly every fighter in the city. But he took Valtan's point. No one would be stupid enough to attack with him here. Valtan could destroy a small army with a wave of his hand.

"Once Uther is on his way," Valtan continued. "I want you to sail to Lux. Perhaps being a governor doesn't suit Philippa as well as she hoped. If we can turn her into at least a spy, that would give us a toehold on the mainland. Once you finish with her, try Kasimir as well. He has a big ego. Losing his crown no doubt grates. One of them will surely turn on Garenland."

"And if neither of them does?" Eddred asked.

Valtan sighed. It was as tired a sound as Eddred had ever heard. "Then we try something else. Good luck."

Eddred nodded and made his way to the city barracks. Good luck was something he desperately needed.

CHAPTER 28

After hemming and hawing for days Otto couldn't put it off any longer. It was time to deal with the Wizards Guild. He had already informed Wolfric and while the emperor wasn't thrilled that Otto was putting himself in danger like this, he did agree that the matter needed to be settled one way or the other.

As he made his way through the city toward their new base, Otto considered his plans. The truth was, until he fully understood their intentions, Otto couldn't do much more than take precautions and hope for the best. He felt slightly helpless and hated it.

When he arrived, he found the warehouse much as he remembered, only the side door had been replaced. The new door was solid oak and fit tight so no light could escape at night. That improvement had to have been Hans's doing. Having the solid soldier back from Rolan was a relief. Otto hadn't realized just how much he counted on the man.

He knocked once and let himself in. The stink of whatever Ulf was working on today filled the space. Though not as bad as in the tavern, it was still far from pleasant. The magical armor was kneeling along one wall ready for action should it be needed. Sin and her thugs were away today. They had discovered shortly after moving in that the warehouse had a tunnel running under it and a trapdoor had been constructed to allow access. Now his spies could come and go without drawing attention. All that remained was for Otto to inscribe a teleportation circle, and it would be all set.

"Lord Shenk?" Hans stepped out from behind his suit of armor and saluted.

The guys had set up cots beside their magical armor, turning the space into a crude barracks. Though far from ideal, it was more comfortable than the old stone armory they'd used as a base on their first mission.

"Get everyone together, we've got a mission."

While Hans grabbed his squad, Otto walked over to the alchemy lab. Ulf was watching a bubbling flask filled with greenish liquid. The ether swirled around his concoction unconnected to any controlling force. It appeared that the process of alchemy activated the ether on its own. Remarkable. There really was so much Otto didn't understand about magic.

Ulf flicked a glance his way. "Can I do something for you, Lord Shenk?"

"I just need you to listen while I brief everyone. You'll need to pass the information along to Allen and Sin. Also, should you need to get a message to the palace while I'm away, I've arranged a password you can give the guards and they'll carry any message directly to the emperor."

Ulf bowed and stepped out from behind the table where he'd been working. A moment later Hans and his men marched up.

"I'm going to meet with the Wizards Guild," Otto said. "My

hope is that they'll see reason and be content with whatever members will join them willingly."

"How likely is that?" Hans asked.

"Not terribly. They have ambitions. I respect that. After all, I'm ambitious as well. The problem is, their ambitions are getting in the way of mine. I can't allow that. Hans, you and your squad will be joining me as bodyguards. Your job will be mainly to keep an eye out for trouble. I'll be focused on magical threats so I might miss something more mundane."

"We are at your service, my lord," Hans said.

Otto handed a slip of paper to Ulf. "Here's the password. Memorize then burn it. I'm counting on the three of you to keep an eye on things while I'm gone. Axel will be by to pick up the next month's supply of the drug if I'm not back by then."

Ulf nodded. "Good luck, my lord."

"Thanks."

Otto led his team out of the warehouse and back to Gold Ward. A few of the rich and powerful gave Hans and his men a second look, but no one complained. Someone traveling with guards wasn't that rare after all.

They found the guildhall as dead as the first time Otto visited. He tried the door and found it locked. Otto rapped twice and waited.

Soon enough the door opened and Cypher peered out at him. "Lord Shenk? This is a surprise. I was beginning to wonder if you were even going to answer our request for a meeting."

"Believe it or not, I do have other matters that require my attention. However, I've settled most of them and have a moment to speak with your guild master. Hopefully we can come to an equitable understanding."

"Absolutely, she'll be delighted to meet you. The primary

guildhall is in Rolan. I'm not sure if the portal has opened yet today so—"

"I can open the portal whenever I need to. Also, I won't be going to your hall. I'm willing to go as far as the capital of Rolan to meet with her on neutral territory, but that's it."

"Are you certain?" Cypher asked. "I think you'd find the guildhall fascinating. We believe it was some sort of a storehouse built by Lord Karonin during her reign. There are a number of wondrous items there. I admit we haven't figured out how to use most of them."

So they'd stumbled onto another armory. If the guild had access to some of his master's magic, that would explain their confidence.

"Perhaps I'll pay a visit after we work out our differences. For now, it would be like stepping into the lion's den. We can meet in Rolan City or not at all."

"Very well. No harm in being cautious I suppose. I'll send her a message before we leave. It'll only take a minute. Please wait outside."

Cypher shut the door on them.

"I don't trust him," Hans said.

"Neither do I. If I did, you wouldn't be here. I'll grab some magical reinforcements when we reach Rolan. Hopefully they won't do anything stupid, but if they do, we'll be ready."

Cypher closed the door and hurried to the secret room in the rear of the guildhall. He settled himself in front of the magic mirror and took deep breaths to settle his racing heart. At long last the time had come. The future of the guild rested on what happened over the next few days. He couldn't mess up.

When he had himself under control, he reached out and poured ether into the mirror. When his master's hooded visage appeared, he said, "Lord Shenk has arrived and agreed to a meeting. He wants to do it in Rolan City, not at the main hall."

"We can work with that. When will you arrive?"

"Soon. We're heading directly for the portal now."

"Tell them I'll need a few days to make the journey. That should get them to lower their guard tonight. The team will arrive after midnight."

"I'll be ready."

The mirror went blank and he stood. Tonight at midnight. That was sooner than he expected, but better to strike fast. Cypher doubted his ability to keep calm for long. He really wasn't cut out for this sort of thing.

Best not to keep Lord Shenk waiting. He sealed the secret room and hurried out into the main office. Outside he found the others waiting patiently.

"Is all well?" Lord Shenk asked.

"Oh yes. The guild master found your suggestion perfectly acceptable. It will take her a few days to arrive though."

"Perhaps we should remain in Garenland until she does," Lord Shenk's bodyguard said. "There's little enough for us to do in Rolan City."

Cypher cursed himself. Of course they wouldn't want to hang around in the city for days. "It is possible she'll arrive sooner. If we're there when she does, the meeting can happen all the quicker."

"I need to discuss a few things with Oskar and check on Corina's training anyway. An extra day or two won't matter." Lord Shenk turned toward the portal. "Let's go."

‿෮

The sun had set in Rolan when Otto and his companions stepped through the portal. After selecting a pair of garrison wizards to act as extra guards, they set out for a nearby inn. Otto considered staying at the fort, but space was tight just for the soldiers.

Days of running around like crazy had left Otto eager for an early turn-in. He'd find Oskar tomorrow and get a detailed report before teaching Corina a new spell. Which new spell he hadn't decided yet, maybe something with fire.

The inn they settled on was called the Proud Stallion. There was nothing remarkable about the place. You could find an inn not much different in most cities in the empire. The Stallion had a typical two-story setup with a common room downstairs and rooms upstairs. Otto bought all the rooms for a week, ordered a meal to be brought up, and went to lie down. Hans fell in beside him while everyone else got a table in the common room. They were lucky that they arrived as early as they did since the inn was nearly empty.

At the top of the steps Otto said, "Join me for a moment, Hans."

As soon as he was inside, he took the portal control rod out of his satchel and held it out to Hans. "I'd like you to hold on to this for me. It's only a precaution, but if things go badly at the meeting, I don't want the guild getting their hands on it."

Hans took the rod and held it like he expected the thing to bite him. "If you're that concerned, maybe we should call this off."

"No. There can only be one master of magic in the empire and I'm it. The guild could make a useful extension of the empire, but I will not share control with anyone. If they want a battle of wills, then by heaven I'll give them one."

"As you say, Lord Shenk." Hans finally tucked the rod inside his tunic.

"There's no one else I trust to protect the rod. Guard it with your life."

Hans straightened and saluted. "I won't fail you, Lord Shenk."

Otto clapped him on the shoulder. "You never have. See you in the morning."

After a mediocre meal of some sort of shredded meat and thick gravy, even his concern about the guild wasn't enough to keep him awake and Otto fell promptly asleep.

It was pitch black in his room when something, he couldn't say what, instinct maybe, brought him awake. A quick glance showed the ether to be more agitated than he'd ever seen it.

He barely had time to register what was happening, when a storm of threads came crashing over him.

Thanks to many months of practice, he raised a barrier at the last moment, but the assault was too much.

His shield shattered in an instant.

There was no pain as he lost consciousness a second time.

CHAPTER 29

Five hundred men, some old enough to be Uther's father and some barely old enough to shave, stood in three lines outside the Markane royal palace. Their mail, weapons, and crimson tabards all looked brand new. Eddred had introduced him to his new team then dashed off toward the docks on some mission for Valtan. Hopefully Eddred would have better luck than the poor merchant they sent to help him.

Not that his own situation was anything to brag about. These so-called soldiers didn't look like they'd ever seen combat. No doubt living on an island protected by the most powerful wizard in the world led to a peaceful life. Pity for them that they were about to get a taste of the real world. Hopefully some of them would survive, or at least not get Uther killed.

"We're ready to move at your command, my lord," said Captain Lancet, the officer in charge of this unit.

What Uther wouldn't have given for a hundred rangers. Oh well, he had to work with what he had. "Our foes are currently burning their way across the western barrier island. We esti-mated their numbers at between one hundred and fifty and two hundred men. What little information I've seen suggests they have no wizards on shore, but that their ships are protected by at least four. As long as we avoid the coast, we should be safe from magic at least."

"We have the numbers advantage then," one of the soldiers said. "These raiders are as good as dead."

Some of the others cheered until Uther silenced them with a glare. "Do not underestimate our enemies. The continent has seen more blood and death than you can imagine. Every one of them has more combat experience than all of you combined. If you're stupid enough to think a mere two-to-one or even three-to-one advantage is enough to ensure a quick victory, you may as well cut your own throat right now before your overconfidence gets someone else killed."

Some of them grimaced, their faces flushed, whether in embarrassment or in anger Uther couldn't say. He hoped anger since that would help them during a fight.

"We have a long march ahead of us. Captain Lancet, move them out."

"Yes, my lord."

The force set out with Uther and Lancet in the lead. No cheering crowds awaited them as they passed through the city toward the eastern gate. A trickle of refugees had been arriving over the last few days and they brought word of the atrocities the raiders had committed. These people, having lived in safety for so long, were stunned by what they heard. Uther doubted the island would ever be the same, even if they drove the enemy off quickly.

Speaking of refugees, a trio of the ragged people, a boy about fifteen and two kids that couldn't have been over ten, shuffled past the soldiers. They had nothing beyond the clothes on their backs. The older boy guided his charges down a side street and out of sight. Perhaps they had family in the city, or maybe they were just looking for a place to sleep.

Uther had heard in passing that a group had been set up to help the people that escaped the barrier islands, but it wasn't anything he'd been involved in. He hadn't even gotten involved when his own people were driven out of their villages and were forced to flee to Marduke. He figured the best thing he could do was stay out of the way and not eat up the emergency supplies.

At the very least, seeing those miserable figures should provide his inexperienced soldiers with a little extra motivation. As they passed under the gate, he suspected they'd need every bit of motivation they could muster.

⌒

Julian sat at the edge of the circle of refugees he'd joined two days before. They had a fire going and a pot of grits was cooking over it. He rubbed the white ring Lord Shenk had given him. Maybe it was his imagination, but he would have sworn it gave off a chill that ran through his entire body. More likely it was just knowing he was wearing an actual magic ring and what it protected him from.

The little skull was tucked safely in his pocket. He didn't want to think what Lord Shenk would do to him if he lost it. And Julian didn't mean Stephan. As crazy as the eldest Shenk brother was, the youngest frightened him far more. How long ago had it been when Otto was little more than the castle joke? He was a failure with a sword. They had all laughed at his efforts in the ring with Sergeant Graves.

No one laughed at him now. When the garrison discussed Otto at all it was in hushed, nervous tones. They had all heard the stories about his fight with Stephan and how he helped capture the spy in Castle Town. But it was the rumors about what he'd done during the war with Straken that really frightened them.

Of course they were just rumors. No doubt highly embellished. That's what they told themselves at least.

"Are you hungry?" a soft female voice asked.

He looked up to see Helen, a woman in her middle thirties with a rather plain, motherly face who had become a sort of leader of the little group, standing over him with a steaming bowl.

Julian accepted and nodded his thanks. He'd been playing the part of a mute to better hide the fact that he was from Garenland. One syllable of his accent and they'd all know he wasn't from Markane. Given what he and his comrades had done since they landed, the refugees would probably tear him apart if they learned the truth.

"I know it's been tough," Helen said. "But don't worry, when we reach the capital tomorrow, we'll be safe behind the walls and with the great wizard to protect us."

She squeezed his arm and returned to handing out bowls. Helen was a kind woman and Julian was glad she wouldn't run into Stephan. On the other hand, what he was going to do wasn't any kinder. He didn't fully understand the magic, but given Lord Shenk's goal, he doubted it would be pleasant.

He ate his tasteless mush and tried not to think about what would happen when they arrived tomorrow.

෧

The walls of Markane's capital appeared in the distance. Julian took a deep breath as they slogged closer. The roads were smooth dirt and the walking easy. The heaviness in their legs came from emotion more than exhaustion.

He'd considered and discarded a dozen stories for when the gate guards questioned him. Just before falling asleep last night, he settled on playing the part of a woodcutter that had escaped because he was out working when the enemy arrived. That should also explain the callouses on his hands.

All around, the other refugees were smiling and slapping each other on the back. The group was small, only eight altogether, and they had become close after their shared suffering. Julian had kept his distance, pretending grief kept him weighed down. The others understood and didn't push, which made his task easier even as his conscience prickled. It wasn't his place to question his orders and that pouch of gold would see his family taken care of for a long time.

The city gate stood wide open as they approached. A pair of archers watched on the battlements above, but no guards waited to question them. Could they really be that sure of themselves? Then again, when the mightiest force in the world protected your city, what did you have to worry about?

Julian was about to answer that question for them. He rubbed his pocket and stepped through the gate into Markane's capital.

The first thing he noticed was the quiet. No hammers pounded steel into shape. The next thing was the smell. The crisp scent of saltwater filled the air, mingling with baker's rolls not too far off.

"Do you have family that will take you in?" Helen asked, startling him.

The rest of the group had already broken up and gone their own ways. Julian nodded and smiled in a way he hoped would seem reassuring.

"Alright. But if you need help, you can find me at the Sweet Delights bakery. My uncle owns it."

Julian bowed his thanks and she hurried off down a cobblestone street to the west. Alone now he focused on his mission. Lord Shenk said any public well would do. He'd drop the skull into the first one he found and get out of there. The last thing he wanted was to end up trapped in a city filled with dead and dying people.

Since he hadn't the slightest idea of the city's layout, Julian turned left and set out. The streets were smooth and free of litter; the buildings, mostly ground-floor businesses with living quarters above. He considered looking for an inn, since there would probably be a stable nearby, then immediately dismissed the idea. An island nation with a seafaring culture wouldn't have much in the way of horses. Maybe if he moved closer to the city center.

He found a side street and turned down it. The path between a pair of buildings was so shadowed that he nearly didn't notice the two men loitering halfway down. They shifted to stand in his path.

"This is our road," the man on the left said. "You want to pass by, you got to pay the toll."

"Ah, it's just another grubby refugee," the second man said. "He probably don't have a pot to piss in."

"Nah," the first man said. "He's got something. See the little bulge in his pocket? Whatever it is, I want it."

Julian hesitated, but if he really wanted the little skull why not let him have it? He reached into his pocket and tossed the skull.

The thug caught it and his hand instantly turned black. A second after that his arm turned as well. The rotten flesh fell to the ground with a splat and soon only black liquid remained. The skull, still perfectly white, as if the sludge wouldn't dare stick to it, rolled away from the dying thug.

As the rot spread to his head and chest, his partner looked from Julian to the barely standing corpse that used to be his companion. He was ready to bolt, Julian could see it in his eyes.

That couldn't be allowed.

Julian pounced, hammering a fist into the thug's stomach and a second to his temple. The man collapsed and Julian leapt on him, pinning him to the ground. The skull was a foot away and he grabbed it.

"Now, you're going to tell me where the nearest well is or I'm going to jam this skull down your throat. What about that?"

"No. Please. Just go to the end of the alley, turn right, two blocks later take a left. There's a little park with a well in the center. Please, just don't do that to me." He was staring at the black puddle that was all that remained of his companion.

"I won't." Julian grabbed the thug by the hair and slammed his head into the stones until he stopped moving. Having seen what happened when the other one touched the skull, he could almost convince himself he'd done a kindness, bludgeoning the fellow to death.

Julian leapt to his feet and hurried away. He didn't want someone to show up and see him standing beside a corpse and a pile of black sludge. A five-minute walk would see his task complete.

Then he could get the hell out of the capital and not a second too soon.

CHAPTER 30

Valtan floated a foot off the floor and let the ether wash over him. He would never admit it, but the continued off-schedule use of the portals was taking a toll on his immortal body. He assumed Otto was doing it on purpose to weaken him or maybe just out of spite. The boy was being affected by the overwhelming amount of ether he'd forced into his body. Right now, he was barely still human and thinking of him as one would be a mistake they could ill afford.

How had it all gone so wrong? How many times had he asked himself that question? Too many it seemed and he still didn't have an answer that pleased him. The only point he could see where he might have averted this catastrophe was at the conclave when the rest of the kingdoms had voted to remove Garenland.

If he had simply refused to deactivate their portal, would this have happened? Probably not as it did, but certainly something would have. And overruling the kings would have sent a message that an Arcane Lord still lorded over them. Valtan had worked too hard and too long for that to happen. He had no desire to rule anyone, though the people of Markane would probably question his honesty about that.

He shook his head and sighed. Done was done, now he had to focus on putting the nations back together. Assuming he could.

Something dark flashed in the ether. Valtan frowned and traced the streak to a place in the city, not all that far from the castle. He couldn't tell exactly what it was, but the magic had a familiar feel, like his old mentor Amet Sur. Of course the ancient necromancer had been gone for centuries, but that didn't mean something nasty hadn't been left behind. Or that Otto hadn't gotten his hands on it.

Either way, Valtan needed to investigate. He became one with the ether and appeared in an alley. A dead body lay beside a pool of thick, dark liquid. Threads of ether shot from Valtan's hand and explored the dark substance.

As best he could tell, it had been a man before the magic Valtan sensed did this to him. It was definitely Amet Sur's power. He'd seen the eldest of the Arcane Lords use something similar to punish those that dared defy him. It was an ugly, horrific way to die.

He searched the area but found no sign of the source. There were magical items that cloaked themselves so you could only feel them when they activated. That no doubt what happened here. Valtan wouldn't sense the item until someone else died.

While he was debating whether to return to the palace or wait where he was, another jagged spike ran through the ether, this one far more powerful than the one that killed the unfortunate man beside him. On the plus side, this made it far easier to track.

Barely a step through the ether brought him to a small park. The slowly dissipating magic was focused on the well that sat in the center of a small, grassy area. There was no one around, but the culprit couldn't have gotten far.

Much as Valtan would have liked to start searching at once, he needed to figure out exactly what had happened. Threads of ether streaked out and into the water. What he found was far worse than he feared. Magical contamination was spreading through the city's water supply. It was already so diffused that he couldn't contain the contamination. Even if he had access to his full power, he wouldn't have been able to stop what was happening.

There was no denying Amet Sur's genius, pity he used so much of it to find better ways to kill and destroy. Valtan sometimes regretted what he had to do but banishing Amet Sur to the netherworld was one thing he never felt bad about. Heaven knew what new horrors he would have dreamed up had he lived.

What mattered now was warning the people. Anyone that drank from the water supply would be killing themselves. Valtan gathered the ether around him and used it to project his voice to everyone in the city. "My people, do not drink from the city wells. The water has been tainted with a magical poison. I am working on a solution and will speak to you again when it's ready."

The people would obey him. They'd been conditioned to do so for uncounted generations. He just hoped that faith and obedience would be rewarded.

He left the park and set out on foot toward the palace. Valtan understood the basics of death magic, but it was one area he had never put much time into. Today he regretted that decision. Countering the poison would take all of his skill and even then, he didn't know if he would succeed.

He rounded a corner and strode into the central plaza where the portal stood shining in the sun. A woman carrying her son staggered and fell, black ooze leaking from her pores.

The poison couldn't have traveled that fast. Did she drink before he sent his warning? there had only been seconds between the magic's activation and when he gave the warning. He looked closer at the dying woman. A faint black thread connected her to the ether.

Valtan frowned and focused his search on the air around him. The ether was now streaked with hair-thin black lines that came from the ground. Now he understood and his despair grew. He had been so focused on the water he hadn't realized what really happened. The water simply acted as a catalyst for the magic. Everywhere the aquifer ran, corrupt energy was rising and killing everyone it touched.

All around him more people staggered out of buildings and collapsed. Valtan reached out through the ether to try and purify them, but the poison acted too quickly and did too much damage. The moment they were touched, the victim was doomed. Valtan had seen some horrible things in his life, but this might be the worst.

And he couldn't do a thing about it.

〇

Julian hurried through the dying city as people melted in puddles of black goo all around him. He tried not to look at them. It was difficult as the screams and moans of the cursed came from every direction. He had known of course that something horrible was going to happen. Death didn't overly bother him. It couldn't if you wanted to make your living as a soldier. But this was death on a scale he couldn't imagine. Cruel and indiscriminate, the skull's magic killed everyone.

He didn't even know how. It wasn't possible that all these people had drunk the poisoned water. Julian shook his head and locked his gaze on the ground in front of him. These people would have been no less dead if they had encountered Stephan and his war band. The means didn't matter if the results were the same.

"Help me," a gurgling voice said.

He looked up to see a boy about ten crawling towards him, his hands already melted along with half his face.

Julian ran.

He had to get out of the city.

How he would escape his memories was another question.

At last he reached the eastern gate where he arrived only to find the portcullis lowered. A squad of guards lay dead in front of it.

"Damn it!" How was he going to get out now?

Julian started walking along the wall and soon came to the stairs leading to the battlements. At the top he looked down over the crenellations. The wall wasn't as high as some city walls, but if he jumped, he was sure to break at least his legs and maybe his neck.

Thinking as he walked, Julian made his way back to the portcullis. He eased over the stone and reached down with his foot.

He still couldn't reach the first gap in the iron bars. His only hope was to hang by his arms and hope that was enough.

Gripping the rough stone so hard his skin tore, Julian felt around with his right foot.

Come on, it had to be there somewhere.

Finally leather touched iron and he eased his weight off his burning hands. His descent didn't get any easier from here. The handholds were thin, nearly too thin for him to work his fingers into. But only nearly. Somehow he managed to get down another rung. From there it was an easy climb to the ground.

For a moment he sat in the grass and took deep breaths. He'd completed his mission. Heaven help him, he'd done it. Now to rejoin Stephan, collect his reward, and hopefully leave this miserable island as soon as possible.

After a few minutes of rest Julian forced himself to his feet and started down the dirt road that led straight to the bridge connecting the main island to West Barrier Island.

He'd barely gone a quarter of a mile when he encountered a family lying in a pool of black ooze on the side of the road. The skull's magic had clearly killed them, but how? They never even arrived in the city. It seemed impossible that the magic should reach this far, but the evidence before his eyes didn't lie.

What would he do if he arrived and found Stephan and the others melted into black muck? Baron Shenk would kill him, assuming he could even find a way back home.

Julian calmed his racing heart. There was no need to jump to conclusions. The islands were separated by a couple hundred yards of ocean. Surely the curse couldn't reach across that. Of course that's what he thought when he escaped the city and see how that turned out.

He shook his head and pressed on. It wasn't like he had any other choice.

CHAPTER 31

Hans woke up with the worst headache in the history of headaches. He'd gotten so drunk once he could hardly see straight and had risen the next day feeling better than this. Certainly the one ale he had the night before hadn't done this to him. The sunlight streaming into his room stabbed his brain through his eyes.

What time was it? Lord Shenk was going to have his head.

He rolled out of bed, splashed some water on his face, and dressed. When he stepped outside, the murmur from the inn's common room reached him. Gritting his teeth, Hans made the short walk to Lord Shenk's room. The door was open and the room empty. The bed hadn't been made, but nobles probably didn't make their own beds anyway. Had he gone downstairs already?

Hans took a step inside and looked around. His gaze locked on to the sword hanging beside the bed. No way would Lord Shenk have left that behind. Something had to have happened.

"Sergeant?"

Hans stepped back out and found one of the garrison wizards standing in the hall. "He's gone."

"We were attacked last night," the wizard said. "A group of wizards, powerful ones, struck us all at once. I didn't even have time to raise a shield. They must have wanted to take him alive."

"Is that why my head feels like a rat is eating my brain? Did the guild do this?"

"Yes on the first question and I assume so on the second. Who else would have the power to do something like this, outside of the war wizards that is, and we aren't trained to take people prisoner."

Hans's jaw bunched. Whatever it took, he would find Lord Shenk and if he found him in less than perfect health, some wizards were going to die. "Wake the others. We'll meet downstairs in ten minutes. There's a wizards guildhall in this city. That's where we'll start."

The wizard saluted and Hans returned to the room. He collected Lord Shenk's mithril sword then searched around for anything else of value. Other than a change of clothes and a coin pouch, there was nothing. He pocketed the coins and left the rest.

He nearly ran down Corina as he stepped out of the room. The girl smiled when she saw him. "Is he up yet? I'm supposed to learn a new spell today."

Hans had never been very good at beating around the bush and she might be of some use in the search. "He was kidnapped last night, we think by the guild."

"They wouldn't dare!"

"So I would have thought, but the truth is before you. Lord Shenk is gone, his weapon and money left behind, and our wizards says magic was involved." Hans shrugged. "What else can we assume?"

Her thin, narrow face scrunched up. "Nothing. How will we find him?"

Hans wasn't surprised that Corina had volunteered to help. She'd become quite attached to their leader. "I'm taking my people to the guildhall to see what they have to say. If you want to join us, you're welcome. But I'd appreciate it if you could run to the fort and fetch Oskar. He might know something."

"I'll be right back." Corina turned and sprinted down the hall.

Hans followed at a more sedate pace. He needed some food and strong tea if he was going to be worth a damn.

They ended up maybe not wasting but spending a full half an hour filling their bellies and clearing their heads. When his breakfast was gone, so was the worst of the headache. His mind focused, Hans led the way out of the inn.

Happily, Corina was jogging down the street toward them, Oskar getting dragged behind her. "There's no sense going to the guildhall," she said. "It's empty."

"I noticed on my morning patrol," said Oskar. "I thought that was strange until Corina told me what happened. There's somewhere else we might check."

"I'm open to suggestions," Hans said.

"The wizard underground kept a secret base out in the plains. They brought Corina and I there when I was on my infiltration mission. I don't know if that's where they took Lord Shenk, but someone there might know where to find him."

"If we plan to take on the guild, we need more wizards," Hans said. "We'll have to take them from Straken and no way will General Varchi let us have them without His Majesty's say-so."

"How long will that take?" Corina asked. She sounded as anxious as Hans felt.

"I don't know, but if we go charging in with what we have now, we'll do no one any good."

CHAPTER 32

West Barrier Island wasn't that much different from Straken. The forest covered the bulk of the land with small villages scattered around connected by dirt roads. For the first time since he arrived, Uther felt at home. One of his men snapped a branch as they thrashed through the woods. Uther bit his tongue to keep from swearing. These were good men, but they knew nothing about woodcraft.

But that wasn't in the cards. There were no rangers now and not much of a Straken. He'd have to make do with these soft islanders. Heaven help them all.

They'd crossed the connecting bridge two days ago and quickly found a group of refugees that pointed them toward the raiders' last known location. They'd reached the burned-out village yesterday and found nothing but charred ruins and bodies, many of them badly used. If that sight wasn't enough to put some steel in the soldiers' spines, then nothing would.

Uther found tracks leading north and they set out, hoping to circle around and set an ambush. That was the plan at least.

Unfortunately there were no roads where he wanted to go and they were forced to travel through the forest. It was easy walking, at least for Uther. For soldiers that had spent their careers stationed in the city, the forest was another world.

For all the problems they'd faced, somehow his force had gotten ahead of the targets and they were now stationed beside the road, ready to strike as soon as the raiders appeared. Perhaps heaven was looking out for them.

Behind him someone cursed and slapped a bug.

Then again, maybe a demon was having a laugh at their expense.

"Quiet," Uther whispered.

There was a little more noisy shifting around followed by silence. Their only blessing was that the enemy didn't have scouts, at least none that Uther had seen. They seemed focused on the villages and nothing else. Uther intended to show them the error of their ways.

A crunch in the distance alerted him to the raiders' approach. A moment later the first rank appeared. They were a rough lot, clearly mercenaries, though a few sported proper uniforms. However their clothes might look, their weapons and armor appeared well cared for. They looked like veterans, exactly the sort of people Uther didn't want to fight with his unblooded troops.

When the enemy was directly opposite them Uther shouted, "Attack!"

He'd barely spoken when the raiders shifted and formed a shield wall to meet their charge.

Instead of the panic he'd hoped for, Uther's troops ran directly into a calm and well-ordered defense. Their blows were met by heavy shields. Three of Uther's men went down to counterstrikes.

The enemy advanced, swords and spears thrusting through gaps in the wall.

Step by step Uther's men were forced back.

He wanted to give the order to retreat, but if they tried to disengage, they'd be cut to pieces.

How could his ambush be going this badly?

The screams of dead and dying islanders filled his ears.

Uther swung, taking the hand of a mercenary at the wrist. The man fell and in desperation Uther lunged through the gap.

He found himself face to face with a huge blond man who swung a longsword with enough force to split Uther in half.

Luckily he turned the blow aside.

That brief exchange had pushed them behind the enemy advance. Uther eyed his opponent warily. This was a man who knew how to fight. One mistake would see Uther dead in short order.

"Lord Shenk!" one of the raiders called. "Are you well?"

"I'm fine, Captain," the blond man said. "Finish these fools so we can get back to work."

"Shenk?" Uther asked. "You must be related to Axel Shenk."

The blond man smiled a cruel smile. "If you know my younger brother, then you must be Prince Uther. I was told you'd fled here, but assumed you'd be hiding behind Valtan's robe."

Uther forced his anger aside. He could make no mistakes with this monster. He raised his sword to high guard and Shenk matched him.

They came together with a massive crash. His opponent was strong, strong enough to be from Straken. Uther was as skilled with the blade as anyone in his country, but he wasn't ashamed to admit this might be an opponent beyond him.

Blow after heavy blow rained down on Uther and Shenk

showed no signs of slowing. Uther spun away from a thrust and countered high, slicing across his opponent's cheek and opening a shallow cut.

Shenk grinned. "First blood, well struck. I see why you gave Axel so much trouble."

Uther didn't waste words talking.

He charged.

He might as well have run into a brick wall for all the blond Garenlander moved. Swords locked, they shoved and jostled for advantage.

In a battle of pure muscle, Uther was in trouble. Seconds after they locked blades, Shenk hurled him ten feet. Uther landed flat on his back, the air rushing out of him.

Shenk advanced as he wheezed for breath.

Uther made it to his knees before death stood directly over him. "You fought well. Just not well enough."

The longsword went up.

Before it could fall Shenk staggered. Captain Lancet stood behind him. The leader of Markane's soldiers was bloody from head to foot. His armor had been smashed open on the right side and he held his arm tight to his body.

"Run, Prince Uther. I'll hold him here."

Shenk got his feet under him and snarled. "I think not."

"Go!" Lancet shouted. "You're no use to Lord Valtan dead."

It seemed to be Uther's fate to have others die in his place. He ran, back the way Shenk's force had come. He silently swore that no matter what he would make Garenland and the Shenk family in particular suffer.

⟲

S tephan hammered the hilt of his longsword into the side of the head of the idiot that dared come between him and his prey. The soldier collapsed in a bleeding heap. He turned but found Uther gone.

"Damn it!" He kicked the soldier hard in the ribs.

No wonder Axel had trouble. Uther was skilled and slippery as an eel. Lucky for Uther, there was only one place he could run, the main island. They needed to get to the bridge and cut him off. At least the battle appeared to be over. A few mercenaries were finishing off injured Markane soldiers but otherwise the battlefield was silent.

"Jost. We need to move."

"Yes, Lord Shenk." Jost quickly got his men together.

While he was busy, Stephan put his blade on the dying man at his feet and pushed it into his gut. The soldier moaned and writhed as he twisted. His pain soothed Stephan's anger. He would find Uther and bring his head back to Garenland. Father could use it as a decoration, or maybe send it to the emperor for the great reward his brother mentioned. Otto had made it clear they wanted the prince dead and Stephan would be happy to oblige his youngest brother.

Two minutes later the raiders were formed up and ready to move. Luckily they'd left the loot behind in a wagon at the last village. Dragging it along behind them was a pain and there was no one left alive to steal it anyway.

"Status, Jost?"

"Five dead and fifteen wounded. I don't know where Uther found this lot, but I doubt they'd ever swung a sword in anger before."

Considering they were outnumbered better than two to one, that was a miracle. Or as Jost suggested good luck that their opponents had zero experience fighting. They set out at a quick march for the bridge. It wasn't hard to figure out how to get there, all the tracks in the road ran that way. People weren't fleeing toward Stephan's mercenaries after all.

They marched for hours, passing through a pair of empty villages on their way. Word must have preceded them since there wasn't a soul in sight. Stephan made a mental note to stop and loot them on the way back. It wasn't as much fun, but looting an empty village was less risky than fighting. If the locals left in a hurry, there had to be something valuable to grab. They had a fair haul so far, but he wanted everything he could get.

They paused for a rest at a crossroad when a voice coming down the left-hand road shouted, "Lord Shenk!"

Stephan turned to find the man that volunteered to carry Otto's magic weapon to the capital hurrying toward them. What was his name? Something with a J. Julian, that was it.

Julian stopped and bowed as he gasped for breath. "Thank heaven I found you before you crossed the bridge. You can't go to the main island. Only death waits there."

"You completed your mission?" Stephan asked.

"Yes, and it was worse than you could imagine. People just melted. Everyone in the city died then the rest of the people on the main island. It's a charnel house over there. We should leave. I doubt the magic will have come this far if it hasn't already, but—"

"Calm down, man." Stephan tried to make sense of Julian's report.

He knew the weapon was supposed to wipe out the city, but this sounded like more than what Otto described. Did his brother not know the extent of what he set loose or did he just figure the city and the island were basically the same?

Stephan had no answers and dying from some stupid out-of-control magic didn't suit him at all. Julian was right. It was time to cut their losses. They'd grab everything they could on the way back to their landing site and signal the ships for pickup. Someone else could hunt down the runaway prince.

"Time to go home, men," Stephan said.

Julian looked so relieved Stephan feared he might weep. Whatever he saw, it must have been truly horrible. It seemed Otto hated Valtan more than Stephan thought. Probably best to keep that in mind before he bothered his little brother again.

CHAPTER 33

Otto wasn't sure how long he'd been stuck in his miserable little cell, he assumed a day or so since he'd eaten twice. He thought he knew what it meant to be bored, but sitting here, with no one to talk to and nothing to do made traveling with the army seem like the most glorious of adventures. Somehow the bars even cut off his access to the ether. When the door at the far end of the hall opened, he was almost relieved to see his captors.

The leaders of the guild stood facing him. They were a grim lot except the stupid one who grinned like he was enjoying himself. Otto would take particular pleasure cutting that smiling face off his skull.

"Time to begin your adjustments." Cypher took the key out and opened the cell door.

Otto stayed seated on his narrow cot.

"Don't make me drag you out of there," the big man said.

Otto still didn't move. Damned if he was going to make this easy for them.

"Have it your way." The stupid one stepped into the cell.

"Easy Tal, we need him in one piece," Cypher said.

"I'm not going to break anything, just bruise him a little so he knows who's in charge." Tal stepped into the cell.

Otto lunged across the space and slammed his elbow into Tal's stomach with all his weight behind it.

The air rushed out of Tal and he doubled over. Otto grabbed him by the hair and slammed him to the floor.

He managed to hammer Tal's face into the stone three times before the others dragged him off. The idiot groaned so unfortunately Otto hadn't killed him. But he did make a point.

"That wasn't necessary," Cypher said. He had Otto's right arm in a firm grip.

"I disagree. You think you can kidnap me, cut me off from my magic, and mess with my mind and there won't be consequences? Maybe this is all I can do, but heaven help me, if I can make you bleed, I will."

"Perhaps leaving him in the cell cut off from the ether has driven him mad," Esmay said.

"No, I think he just has a terrible personality," said one of the ones Otto didn't know, the younger one. "Let's get him strapped in so we can begin."

Otto didn't fight them as he was led out of the cell block and down a different hall. Twice he tried to touch the ether and both times one of the others smashed his threads as soon as they formed. At least he could touch it again. That was comforting even if it was useless at the moment.

They ended up in a stone room with a single high-backed wooden chair. Leather straps had been added to the arms, legs, and back. Otto soon had them wrapped around his wrists, ankles, and neck. Tal had somewhat gathered himself and joined them. He looked like he wanted to beat Otto to a pulp.

Blood covered his face, his nose was bent to the left, and a tooth had fallen out.

All and all, Otto thought Sergeant Graves would be pleased with his effort.

Who was he kidding? No doubt he'd be criticized for not killing the man. It was a lack of strength, not effort, that saved Tal.

His captors formed a circle around him with Esmay directly in front. The petite woman frowned at Otto. "Please don't resist me. This magic can be painful if you fight it."

If they thought a little pain was enough to convince him to fold, they knew nothing. "Where's your master? I assumed she'd be handling this herself."

"Her talents lie elsewhere," Cypher said. "Mental alterations are Esmay's specialty."

"Just look straight ahead and try to relax." Esmay conjured a disk of spinning light.

Otto clamped his eyes shut.

A moment later a thick thread of ether forced them open. When he tried to destroy it, his magic was blocked. As best Otto could tell, the three blocking him were using around twenty-five threads between them. If he used his full power, he could overwhelm them, but the other two would certainly jump in. Better to conceal his maximum power until he could make use of it.

Otto drew his power back, this time turning it inward and wrapping his brain in a protective bubble. Hopefully they wouldn't hit too hard for fear of damaging his mind. Turning him into a drooling idiot certainly wouldn't help their cause.

"He's formed a barrier," Cypher said. "What should we do?"

"Nothing," Esmay said. "Once the wheel has him hypnotized, he'll lose concentration and the barrier will fall naturally. Just be patient."

Of course what Otto knew and apparently they didn't, was that because he knew exactly what they were trying to do, he was almost impossible to hypnotize. He defocused his eyes until the wheel was little more than a spinning blob and focused on his breathing. Breathe in, breathe out, focus on the barrier and nothing else.

It was like meditation and hours passed, he didn't know how many, until finally the wheel vanished along with the pressure holding his eyes open. He blinked his dry, scratchy eyes until they stopped hurting.

"You accomplished nothing," Tal said.

"I don't understand," Esmay said. "I've used this spell before and no one has lasted longer than fifteen minutes before going under."

"Maybe you need more practice," Otto said.

"Let's take him back." Cypher moved to block Tal who had taken a step toward Otto. "Clearly we need a different strategy."

The walk back was harder after being locked in place for heaven only knew how long and Otto's legs complained with every step. It was with relief that he collapsed on his cot. The others left until it was just him and Cypher.

"You're only making this harder on yourself," Cypher said. "You'll break eventually."

"Maybe, but I promise you my people are looking for me. I just need to hold out until they arrive."

"No one will find this place. It's hidden by magic."

"You found it and so will my people. I will get out of here eventually and when I do, I'm going to kill you all in the most painful manner I can think of."

Cypher shook his head and walked away.

Smug bastard. He'd pay. They all would.

◯

It took longer than Hans wanted to get back to Garenland, but since Lord Shenk wasn't there to open the portal for them, they were forced to wait until Rolan's turn in the rotation. At least Emperor Wolfric, who had been waiting for word, granted Hans an immediate audience.

To say that he had been upset to learn that his chief advisor and best friend was missing and presumed kidnapped by the Wizards Guild would be putting it mildly. Despite Lord Shenk's warning he appeared to have assumed nothing would actually happen.

The emperor had written a letter giving Hans full authority to seize whatever resources he needed to rescue Lord Shenk. Even General Varchi hadn't argued when Hans took a dozen wizards to help with the hunt. All of them jumped at the chance to repay Lord Shenk for what he'd done for them. He'd hoped to enlist Master Enoch as well, but when he paid a visit to Franken Manor, he'd been told the wizard was off on a personal matter.

So, a man shorter than he would have preferred, Hans had returned to Rolan. Oskar and Corina had taken the lead and now they were riding through the plains toward the wizard underground's base, one of them anyway. He doubted they'd find Lord Shenk there, but maybe they could find some information.

"We're almost there," Oskar said.

Hans looked around at the endless sea of waving grass.

There was nothing here remotely resembling civilization. "Where?"

"He's right, sir," said one of the wizards, a middle-aged man named Draken who served as the unofficial leader of the group. "The ether is different up ahead. It's subtle. I wouldn't have even noticed if I hadn't known to look."

"The underground is good at hiding," Oskar said. "They needed to be to survive."

Twenty paces further on Oskar stopped. The grass around him had been disturbed and Hans didn't think it was by animals. There was something here for sure.

"Is there any way to make whatever they're hiding visible?" Hans asked.

The wizards huddled and had a quiet conversation before Draken said, "I believe we can. One moment."

Hans glanced at his squad and nodded left and right. They dismounted and spread out, ready for anything.

The wizards all raised their hands. For once Hans wished he could see what they were doing.

Whatever they did, it worked. A sod longhouse appeared as though out of a thick fog. The only wooden part was a frame with a door set in it. It must have taken a lot of power to make something so big vanish.

"I don't sense any traps." Draken squinted. "I also don't sense any people. I'd say this place is abandoned."

"They had to know we'd come searching for Lord Shenk and that Oskar could lead us here." Hans shook his head, disappointed but not surprised. "Let's look around anyway. If they left in a hurry, they might have missed something."

One of the wizards pointed and the door was smashed open. Nothing exploded or shot arrows at them. Of course, that didn't mean there were no traps inside, but that might just be Hans's natural pessimism talking.

The inside of the longhouse had been cleaned out. No furniture, no supplies, no gear, no nothing. They didn't leave so much as a clue as to where they might have gone.

"Damn it!" Hans wanted to punch someone, preferably Cypher. "This was a complete waste of time. Now what are we supposed to do?"

"It wasn't a complete waste," Oskar said, a thoughtful, distant look on his face. "Our wizards now know what to look for. If they spot something that looks like the magic hiding this place, we'll know we've found another."

"But we can only search a small area," Draken pointed out. "It will take forever if we have to search the entire country."

Corina moved a little way off by herself and studied the floor. "This is different," she said at last.

Hans joined her and a moment later so did Oskar. There was nothing remarkable about the patch of dirt floor, at least not that Hans could see.

"What do you mean?" Oskar asked.

"Do you remember the last time we were here? There was an outline. I remember because it was the only part of the floor that was smooth. It's gone now."

"Draken, check it out." Hans motioned the wizard over.

"She's right," Draken said at last. "There's something here. The ether is different from the concealment spell, but magic was worked here and not that long ago. Let's see what they're hiding."

Hans paced as the wizard did his thing. He hated relying on others, but when magic was involved there was no choice. Draken walked slowly down the length of the longhouse. At the far end he turned and started back.

Having the others help seemed like it would speed things up, but maybe they'd just get in the way. Hans didn't know enough about magic to make a suggestion.

Halfway back to the entrance Draken stopped. "Here. The wizards used magic to hide an underground chamber and reinforce it so no one could break in, but they missed a patch of earth. We can dig down into it right here."

"Grab the trenching tools," Hans said.

Fifteen minutes later they had a five-foot diameter hole punched through the floor. The chamber beyond was pitch black. One of the wizards sent a light down revealing another room just as empty as the longhouse.

Hans cursed the universe. They'd wasted all that time for nothing.

"I see something." Corina jumped down into the hidden room.

She ran over to the side of the wall and knelt, digging with her bare hands. Soon she came up with a cloth-wrapped bundle. How had she spotted that from so far away? Hans had pretty good eyesight, but he hadn't noticed a thing.

"Someone want to help me out of here?" Corina asked. A rope was lowered and she climbed out. "I think it's a book."

They unwrapped the bundle and sure enough it held a small notebook like you might use for a diary. With nothing better to go on they all gathered around and started to read.

It wasn't until almost the end that they found something relevant. It seemed the journal belonged to a teenage girl that the underground rescued. She spent some time at the longhouse and helped out in the storage room.

Most of the entries were mundane, day-to-day things, but one day she overheard some of the higher-ups talking about an important meeting with the leader of their group at a place they called the guildhall. That name implied that the underground always thought about themselves as a guild even before they officially became one.

The important bit was a description of the meeting place, a dead section of prairie that all the herdsmen avoided. Hans looked up. "That's great, but how are we going to find one patch of dead grass out here?"

"Easy," Corina said. "My family were cattle traders. We heard all the stories and the Dead Spot was always a favorite. Everyone liked to speculate how it came to be and why it scared the cattle. Anybody want to bet magic was involved? Anyway, I know right where it is."

Hans grinned. "Let's get out of here."

As they were leaving, he touched Corina on the shoulder. "He'll be proud of you. We never would have gotten this far without your help."

Corina beamed and practically skipped out of the longhouse. Hans followed her with a more sober expression. Finding Lord Shenk was one thing, rescuing him quite another.

CHAPTER 34

Cypher set a bowl of tasteless gruel on the cell floor along with a glass of water before leaving Otto alone with his so-called meal. Day in and day out for hours at a time they tried to hypnotize and manipulate Otto's mind and they continued to fail. On the one hand this was good since Otto had no desire to become the guild's puppet, on the other, he feared what they might do when their patience ran out.

The only thing he was certain of was that it would be unpleasant. He gathered up his meager repast and settled on the edge of his cot to eat. Not that he was especially hungry, but he knew he had to keep his strength up, so he'd be ready when his moment came.

He took one bite and immediately stopped. Something was wrong. The food tasted different, not better by any means, but something spicy had been added. He knew enough about poisons to know that they were often added to strong-flavored dishes so the target wouldn't realize what they were eating.

That was one of the reasons Father always ate the same food, so he would recognize if something was off.

It would seem his captors had decided to up the stakes. Otto set the bowl down and eyed his water. Going for a while without food would be unpleasant but doing without water was another thing altogether. He didn't have a proper filter, but maybe he could improvise something to take the worst of it out.

Otto soaked his shirt with the water then wrung it out into the cup and drank. After a few minutes he still felt okay. Either his trick had worked or the water wasn't poisoned. He shrugged and put the cup and bowl back beside the door.

Fifteen minutes later Cypher returned, looked from the still-full bowl back to Otto, and shook his head. "You're determined not to make this easy. How did you know?"

"That you poisoned my food? Why else would you have suddenly given it some actual flavor? You people seem to think I'm an idiot. Rest assured, I'm not."

"If you would only see reason. We are not your enemy."

Otto made a show of looking around at the cage in which he found himself. "Right. Clearly we're on the same side."

"Have it your way. You've got a visitor. Maybe he can persuade you to do the right thing." Cypher collected the bowl and cup and left. A moment later Master Enoch took his place.

Otto leapt to his feet. "Master! What are you doing here? How did you find this place?"

"I was a member of the underground, remember? I came here once just before I left. There was nowhere else I could imagine them taking you. The guild master is still willing to release you if you swear to join the guild and encourage all the other wizards to do so as well."

Otto snorted. "After all the times I've refused, why would she believe me now?"

"There's an artifact. You hold it and speak your oath. It will tell if you're sincere or lying." Enoch put his hands on the bars, his tattered brown robe sliding down over his skinny arms. "They're getting impatient. I fear they may soon resort to extreme measures."

"Then get me out of here. You can still use magic on that side of the bars. Opening the lock should be simple."

Enoch shook his head. "The ether won't touch either the bars or lock. Only the proper key or I suppose a lock pick will open the door. And even if I could free you, it would only lead to further conflict. The guild is right about one thing: the wizards of the world need to stand together. As a member, you'd be second in power only to the guild master. You'd be in a position to influence their decisions."

Otto couldn't quite believe what he was hearing. "Are you taking their side? After everything I've done for you. I protected you from Stephan and gave you a place of honor teaching the war wizards. I offered to let you stay in my home and this is how you repay me. I thought you were more loyal."

"My loyalty is to all wizards, not just you. I am grateful for everything you've done for me, Otto, truly, but the only way this division among wizards can end is for you to accept the guild's position."

Otto went cold inside. He understood now what he needed to do. His former master had given him one last lesson. "Perhaps you're right. Maybe my ego has prevented me from seeing the path of the greater good. Tell your friends I will consider their proposal and give an answer tomorrow."

Enoch smiled. "I know you'll do the right thing. You were my finest pupil, Otto. I never doubted you for a moment."

"Thank you, Master. Will you do me a favor?"

"Anything."

"If I give the oath, will you stand with me?"

"I'd be honored." Enoch bowed. "Excuse me. They're waiting to hear your response. I'm sure the guild master will be pleased."

Otto nodded and sat back down. He'd give them an answer all right. One they'd never forget.

～

Enoch allowed himself a moment to breathe after leaving the cell block behind. Seeing Otto like that, locked up, dressed in wrinkled, dirty, sweat-stained clothes saddened him. That his prize pupil should end up in such a wretched state...

He sighed. Apparently even the nobility had their limits. The worst part had been when Otto accused him of betraying his faith. Enoch considered that unfair in the extreme. What he was doing was for the greater good, something all wizards needed to keep in mind. It wasn't personal. He thought of Otto almost like a son. As a parent, sometimes it was necessary to correct a wayward child.

When he had himself fully under control, Enoch walked down the long dark corridor and up the stairs to the main level. Cypher was waiting and guided him silently to the meeting hall where the guild master and the rest of the leaders waited. He moved to stand at the foot of the long table while Cypher took his place near the guild master at the head.

The guild master turned her cowled head in his direction. "Well, did he see reason?"

"Otto asked for a day to consider, but I believe the poison frightened him. I think you'll get the answer you desire."

"He seemed more angry than frightened to me," Cypher said.

"Of course he did," Enoch said. "You don't think he'd show weakness to someone he considers his enemy, do you? Otto has been trained his whole life to show no weakness and I assure you his father was a thorough teacher. But I'm his friend and mentor, there's no reason for him to hide his true feelings with me. He will make the oath and it will be true."

"You're a blind fool," Tal said. "There's no way a little poison that he didn't even eat was enough to break him. I don't know what the little bastard is up to, but he's up to something."

Enoch looked around the meeting room at the six wizards gathered there. "What could he be up to? Otto is outnumbered and overpowered. The six of you are some of the strongest wizards on the continent. With me here as well he has no chance of escaping. His only way out of here is to make a deal and he knows it. The next day will simply be Otto convincing himself of that truth."

"So are you saying that if he tries something foolish, you'll help us against your former student?" the guild master asked.

Enoch nodded. "I will. For the good of wizardkind this standoff needs to end. The guild is the stronger force therefore Otto must be the one to give way. It is as simple as that."

The guild master stood from her place at the head of the table. "If you're that confident, we will give him his day to think. Tomorrow, we shall have to hope he makes the correct decision."

Hans wasn't going to lie, a patch of dead grass in the middle of the prairie wasn't all that impressive. Corina had led them here with no trouble just as she promised. The problem was, no one knew what to do now. The wizards were all staring off into space, looking at whatever it was wizards looked at. Hans and his squad sat on their horses and kept their hands close to the hilts of their swords.

Corina nudged her mount over beside him. "Do you think he'll be okay?"

"Lord Shenk is tough, especially for a noble. He's been through a war and an insurrection and came through them without a scratch. Besides, if the guild wanted him dead, they'd have killed him at the inn and left his body for us to find in the morning. No, they want something from him and they need him alive to get it."

"You have a lot of faith in him. Why?"

That was a good question. Hans wasn't sure himself. He'd always served King Wolfric loyally, but if he was forced to choose, his loyalty now belonged entirely with Lord Shenk. The fact that he was devoted to the empire and Wolfric made that easier. Hans wasn't even sure when it happened, but it did.

"He's always treated me with respect and loyalty. While he can be scary at times, especially when he's in a bad mood or someone is making his work difficult, I've never truly feared for my life when I was with him. Speaking of which, he saved my life on more than one occasion and never asked for anything in return. He's a good friend to have."

"I think so too." Corina smiled as if remembering something nice. "Lord Shenk has taught me a lot. He does scare me sometimes too, but not that much. I want to see him again and keep learning. I want to be his apprentice for real."

"If you help rescue him, there's a good chance he'll grant your wish."

Draken guided his horse over beside them. "We can't find anything. The ether is as calm and smooth as I've ever seen it. If something is hidden around here then the magic is beyond us."

"Damn it!" Hans stared at the sky. "Come on, my lord, give me a sign. We're close, we just need something to point the rest of the way."

Hans wasn't sure what he expected, but the sky remained clear and blue, as indifferent to his request as the earth.

"We'll have to search—"

His order was cut off by an explosion. Ahead of them a three-story tower shimmered into view about a hundred yards away. A moment later a body came flying out the hole that was blasted in its side.

"How the hell did you miss that?" Hans demanded as he thumped his horse in the ribs.

Draken shook his head and hastened to keep up.

As they raced toward the tower Hans said a silent prayer that the body that fell to earth wasn't Lord Shenk's.

CHAPTER 35

When Cypher and the other leaders came for him the next day, Otto was ready. He'd spent his time meditating and focusing his mind on what was to come. Whether as the victor or a corpse, he would be free today.

"Well," Cypher said. "Enoch told us you'd have a decision for us today."

Otto stood. "I do. I'm ready to swear the oath. I still think forcing wizards to join is a mistake, but I'm done wasting time arguing with you. We'll find some way to make this work."

Tal glared but the others appeared relieved. No doubt they were as eager to leave this place as Otto.

"You might have saved us a lot of time and given your oath when I first asked you." Cypher pulled out a key and unlocked the cell door. "Come on, guild master's waiting."

Otto crossed the cell, making no aggressive moves or any attempt to touch the ether. He walked calmly down the hall and up the steps to the meeting room where Enoch and the guild master waited. A new item had been added to the decor, a steel tripod holding a black orb as big as Otto's fist. That would be the artifact. The size was a relief. He'd feared something huge he'd have to grasp with both hands. But this would suit his needs perfectly.

"I'm pleased you finally saw reason," the guild master said.

"Sitting in a cell and getting mentally tortured will focus your thinking. I'm doing no one any good here. Add to that not being able to eat for fear of getting poisoned and giving in to your wishes seemed the least bad option. So what do I do?"

"Your enthusiasm is underwhelming, but then again I've never met a nobleman that took losing well." The guild master took the orb from its stand, walked over to Otto, and handed it to him. For something so small the orb was quite heavy. "The process is simple. Hold the orb, swear to serve the guild and obey the guild master. If your promise is true, the orb will turn white. If not, it will stay black. Assuming it turns white, we'll have you back to Rolan City in two days."

Otto hefted the orb and nodded as if composing his thoughts. He glanced around and found Cypher to his immediate right, about ten feet away.

"I swear," Otto began. "To see every one of you dead by my hand."

Before the orb could turn white, he threw it as hard as he could at Cypher. It struck dead center in his forehead.

Otto called every thread he could muster.

"What are you doing?" Enoch reached for the ether to try and stop him.

The moment he did, Otto sent a thread into his mithril ring.

Enoch's magic became Otto's to control. He forged a tentacle out of it and lashed out at Esmay, taking her by surprise and sending her flying across the room.

That was three down and four to go.

He summoned an ethereal barrier just as a storm of threads came roaring in at him.

His shield held, but only just.

Enoch's power lashed out again at Otto's command, this time a lightning bolt hammered into Tal's side and sent him crashing into the table.

Taking no pains to spare his softly moaning former master, Otto wove a net and hurled it at the guild master.

She shredded it but left herself open.

He wove, all thirty-three threads he could muster, and hurled the most powerful bolt of lightning he'd ever summoned.

The guild master went flying through the air, slammed into the wall and was blown through it.

Otto spun, exhausted but determined to finish the fight.

The leaders of Lux's and Rolan's guildhalls were gone. With a thought he sent threads searching but found no signs of them.

There must be a secret way out. Much as Otto hated loose ends, he was in no shape to go hunting for them now.

He released Enoch's magic and the old man collapsed like a puppet with its threads cut. That was exactly how Otto felt, but he kept his feet by sheer will.

"Lord Shenk!" Hans came running in with the rest of his squad, Corina, and a dozen wizards behind him. "Are you all right?"

"I'm alive."

Corina nearly tackled him to the ground she hugged him so hard. "We were so worried."

He gave her a pat on the back before working free of her grasp. "Are those four still alive?"

The squad went to check. Esmay, Tal, and Enoch all survived. Cypher's skull was crushed.

"Did you see the door on your left?" Otto asked.

"Yes, my lord," Hans said. "We need to get you to a healer."

"Time enough for that later. On Cypher's person you'll find a key. Take it and lock the survivors in the cells you'll find beyond that door. Quickly, before they wake up. War wizards, search the tower for a secret door. Two of them escaped during the battle. Touch nothing. Heaven knows what traps they might have left."

"Even Master Enoch?" Hans asked.

"He betrayed me, Hans. After everything I've done, the ungrateful old man sold me out to the guild. He'll get what's coming to him. They all will."

Soon enough only Otto, Hans and Corina remained in the meeting hall. The three of them settled into undamaged chairs and Corina asked, "What happened?"

Otto told them everything up until the moment he hurled the oath sphere into Cypher's head. "It's funny. If Enoch hadn't betrayed me and come here, there's no way I would have escaped."

"What's the plan now?" Hans asked.

Otto sighed and rubbed his eyes. "I'm going to leave a small force here, two of your men and the wizards. They'll keep an eye on the prisoners until I return and if we're lucky, maybe the escapees will try and sneak back to rescue them. It's not likely, but who knows. I need to talk to Wolfric and find out what happened in my absence. How long have I been prisoner here anyway?"

Hans cocked his head and counted on his fingers. "Two weeks, I think. I'm sorry it took us so long to find you. Truth is, we'd still be looking if not for this one's keen eyes."

He turned to Corina who smiled. "I'm glad I could help."

"You've certainly proven more reliable than my former teacher. Reliable enough to be a proper apprentice."

"Really? You mean it?" She looked so happy Otto couldn't help smiling himself.

"I mean it. But you know that with my work, there will be times when I have to do things and you won't be able to join me. You'll have to be patient and follow orders. Can you do that?"

"I can. I'll do anything you want; I promise."

"Then when we get home, I'll find you a mithril ring and make it official."

One of the wizards returned and said, "We couldn't find any secret doors, my lord. The tower appears secure."

"Very well. You'll be standing guard here for a little while so see if you can find their living quarters." The wizard saluted and left. Otto turned to Hans and said, "Choose two men to remain behind. The rest of us need to get moving."

"Are you certain you're up to it?" Hans asked.

"Not in the least, but I need to get back. Heaven knows what's gone wrong in my absence."

CHAPTER 36

I t took three days to ride from the guild's hidden base back to Rolan City. A quick trip through the portal brought them the rest of the way to Garenland. Before they left, he'd taken a moment to examine the guild master's body.

She was a rather plain woman under the cloak she always wore. He found a pair of magical items, a ring set with a black onyx and rune-covered amulet, on her person. He'd claimed them for later study. The body he left where it was for the crows.

When they finally reached home, Otto was so exhausted he went straight to the mansion and right to sleep. At least he assumed he did. The trip through the city was a blur. Only Hans's steady hand on his arm kept him moving in the right direction.

Now, twenty hours later, rested and fed, cleaned up and dressed in fresh clothes, his mithril sword back at his side and the portal control rod tucked safely in a hidden pocket of his cloak, Otto made his way across Gold Ward to the palace.

As he walked his gaze darted everywhere. The odds of anyone from the guild attacking him here were tiny, but not zero. He didn't intend to be taken prisoner again. Fortunately, he reached the outer gate without incident and the guards saluted before waving him in.

It was good to be back in familiar territory. There was still work to be done. It seemed like there was always work that needed to be done, but that would keep for another day or two while he recovered his full strength. Seeing Wolfric, on the other hand, most certainly would not keep. According to Hans, the emperor had been quite anxious when he learned of Otto's capture.

Some of the servants must have sent word of his arrival ahead because when he reached the throne room doors Captain Borden was waiting. "Lord Shenk. His Majesty asked me to escort you to his private dining room. This way, please."

Otto didn't need an escort, he'd been there plenty of times, but perhaps Wolfric meant it as some sort of honor. Either that or he just didn't want Otto wandering off before he got a chance to talk.

It felt like someone had cleared the halls ahead of them as there wasn't a soldier or servant to be seen. If they had wanted to try and assassinate him, this would be the perfect place. Otto gave a mental shake of his head. He couldn't be so paranoid. Here, at least, he was safe.

The door to the dining room was nothing special, you could easily walk past the oak door without giving it a second look. Which was exactly the point. No one would expect to find the emperor behind such a plain door.

Borden opened the door and Otto stepped through. Wolfric sat at a small, mahogany table, a silver tray covered with wine glasses in front of him. He was dressed simply in black and gold, his heavy robe of state tossed over an extra chair behind him.

Wolfric poured two glasses of wine, stood, and offered one to Otto. "Congratulations on your safe return. You had me worried, old friend."

Otto took the glass and they clinked. After a sip and a sigh Otto said, "I am sorry about that. The guild's actions were more aggressive than I anticipated. On the plus side, their leader is dead as is her second-in-command. Three others have been taken into custody. I will deal with them shortly. Two escaped and I assume the other members are scattered around the empire. As long as they behave themselves, I'm inclined to let them be."

Wolfric nodded and took a drink. "I'm happy to follow your lead on the matter."

"Thank you. How are the merchants behaving? I didn't take time to speak with Edwyn before I came here."

"I spoke to him myself. While you were gone, I paid a visit to Annamaria. I've really been terrible about neglecting her. We're not as close as we used to be, but I still consider her a friend."

Otto's throat tightened and he set his glass down before Wolfric could notice his shaking hand. "How did that go?"

"Good. Your daughter is adorable. The nobles are always nagging me to find a wife and sire an heir. Having seen the little angel, I'm seriously considering taking their advice. You're a lucky man."

Otto smiled and relaxed. Annamaria had been on her best behavior. Good, he wouldn't have to punish her when he returned home.

Before they could move on to more pleasant topics, someone knocked on the door.

"Damn it!" Wolfric said. "I told Borden I didn't want to be disturbed."

"That implies whatever they want is important. I have little more to report anyway."

"Fine. Enter!"

Borden and a sweat-soaked soldier stepped inside. The soldier bowed and said, "Majesty, Eddred of Markane has just docked in Crystal City. Henry told me to get word to you right away."

"I didn't think Eddred had the stones for a stunt like this," Wolfric said. "It seems I underestimated him."

"I'll go," Otto said. "We need to deal with him sooner or later. With Valtan isolated, Eddred's his best link to the outside world."

"No," Wolfric said. "You still look half dead. You need more rest, that's a royal decree. Order Henry and the city garrison to take him into custody. If he resists, kill him. Whatever they do, Eddred is not to leave the city alive."

"Yes, Majesty." The soldier rushed out. He should be able to make it back to the portal if he hurried.

Otto scowled at being left behind, but Wolfric was right. He needed at least two more days of rest to get back his strength. If he collapsed, only their enemies benefited.

Hopefully once he became an Arcane Lord, his weakness would be a thing of the past.

〇

Eddred could hardly believe he was back in Lux. The docks were largely empty at midday. The fishermen would be back near dark, but Eddred hoped to be long gone by then. Every moment he remained on land increased the odds he'd be spotted and captured.

As the crew hastened to tie the ship off, he considered how best to approach Philippa. His instructions were to sound her out, but he knew Valtan well enough to understand that he'd be disappointed with anything less than a commitment to fight Garenland, even if it was only in subtle ways. The problem for Eddred was that he had nothing tangible to offer her and Garenland was perfectly capable of killing her and putting a puppet in her place, angry populace be damned.

One of the sailors finished setting the gangplank in position. "We're all set, my lord."

"Good, I hope to be back within the hour. Tell the captain not to get comfortable."

The sailor saluted and Eddred marched down the gangplank with the two wizards that served as his personal guard behind him. The hourglass had flipped and the sands were running. The sooner he could get out of here the better.

"Have you come up with an approach, Majesty?" Lilly, the younger of his guards, asked.

"The only thing I can think of is to tell her the truth and hope she sees things as I do. There's no way I can force the issue and if I try, she may well arrest me on the spot."

"We won't let that happen, Majesty," Adam, the elder wizard, said.

He appreciated the thought, but Markane's wizards studied only defensive magic. It was one of the laws Valtan insisted upon. Their skill at protection made them ideal bodyguards, but poor warriors. If this war was going to drag on, he may have to reconsider that stance. Garenland certainly had no qualms about using offensive magic.

A few locals out for a noon stroll glanced at them as they

passed, but no one approached. There was still no sign of the garrison either. Hopefully they'd arrived without attracting attention. Something had to go Markane's way. Heaven knew they were due for a break.

They reached the Crystal Palace and thankfully found the guards on duty wearing Lux's blue and silver tabards and not black and gold. Both men came to attention.

The elder said, "King Eddred. We weren't told to expect your arrival."

"It was a last-minute decision. I need to speak to Philippa as soon as possible. Could you send a messenger?"

"Certainly, Majesty." The guard glanced at his younger companion and nodded toward the castle. The second guard jogged off leaving them alone outside the gate.

"Is there somewhere out of sight we can wait?" Eddred asked. "I'd prefer not to attract attention if at all possible."

"Too late for that," the guard said. "Didn't you see the lookout following you? Garenland set up a whole network of the little rats. They note every ship coming and going and every person that comes to the palace. I'm afraid Her Majesty hasn't fully earned the trust of our new emperor."

Eddred cursed to himself. He had less time than he thought.

The minutes seemed to stretch to hours as he waited for the messenger to return. Eddred paced and worried, every few seconds he'd check for approaching enemies. He could almost hear their boots on the cobblestones.

After what seemed like half a day but was probably only fifteen minutes, Philippa herself approached the gate with a four-person escort. She looked as lovely as always as she swept toward him in a seafoam-green dress that swirled like a wave around her.

"Eddred, what a nice surprise. Can you stay for lunch?"

"No, I fear I don't have much time. Is there somewhere nearby we can talk alone?"

"We can talk right here." Philippa waved away the guards until it was only the two of them standing just inside the open gate. "What is it?"

"Valtan is determined to resist Garenland's expansion and he wanted to find out whose help we can count on. You and Kasimir are the only rulers still in charge of their land. Will you help us?"

Philippa's smile was bitter. "I'm only a figurehead. They call me governor, but I have no real power. That belongs to the merchants and the wizards. I'm still alive because Wolfric thinks seeing me on the throne pleases my people. You've wasted your time coming here."

Eddred checked again but they were still alone. "I'm not looking for soldiers or war material, I need information. Even a figurehead has ears. Will you pass what information you can to me? Please."

Philippa chewed her lip, clearly torn between wanting to help and wanting to stay alive. "I'll see what I can do. I can promise no more."

"Majesty!" Lilly said. "They're coming."

"Thank you, Philippa. When we figure out a way to contact you, you'll know."

Eddred squeezed her hands before hurrying to join his guards. He really could hear the marching of heavy boots now. The three of them ran deeper into the city. They'd have to make a circle to reach the ship, but that would give them a chance to put some distance between them and their hunters.

The important thing was he had Philippa on his side. That was more than he'd dared hope. It was a small thing, but it lifted Eddred's spirit.

CHAPTER 37

Henry led his force of soldiers and wizards at a quick march toward the Crystal Palace. When his spies brought word that Eddred of Markane had docked, he could hardly believe it. The man had guts if not brains which was certainly not his reputation. The moment word arrived from Garenland to take him into custody or failing that kill him, Henry had set out at the head of a large force of thirty garrison soldiers and four war wizards. He sent another, smaller force to seize control of their ship. There was no way Eddred could escape.

When they reached the Crystal Palace, they found Philippa near the open gate. No doubt she had just finished her visit with Eddred. "He can't have gotten far. Fan out and search. I need to speak with the governor."

Henry left his people to search and strode over to Philippa. The guards knew him and knew better than to try and bar his way. She met Henry's gaze, chin up and proud. He'd met with the former queen on several occasions and she always held herself like she still wielded real power.

"Governor." Henry bowed slightly as protocol required. "What did Eddred want?"

"What makes you think he wanted anything?"

Henry smiled. "I doubt you were standing by the gate because you enjoy the view and I know he was headed this way. What other purpose could he have?"

"He wanted an ally against Garenland. The fool still imagines things can return to the way they were." She gave a disgusted shake of her head. "I told him I had no real power and couldn't help him. You showed up before he could press his case."

Henry assumed she was lying but that wasn't his problem. "Which way did he go?"

She pointed deeper into the city. That made sense, he'd probably try to circle back to his ship. There'd be a surprise waiting for him when he arrived.

Henry left Philippa and hurried over to his team. "Did you find anything? She said he was headed deeper into the city."

"It's impossible to track anyone across cobblestone," the unit commander said.

"Fine. Let's head to the docks. There's no other way for Eddred to escape, not with the portal guard on watch."

The docks were a fair distance from the palace and when they arrived Henry found his advance team exchanging arrows with the crew. The soldiers were crouched behind piles of crates that now resembled pincushions.

Henry stopped well out of bow range and eyed the situation. "Can you reach the ship with magic?"

"Yes, sir," the head wizard said. "A couple fireballs should clear the deck."

Henry nodded. "Do it."

A few seconds later three melon-sized orange globes were hurtling toward the Markane ship.

They exploded on impact sending flames rushing everywhere. Men screamed and leapt over the rail. No counterspells came their way which argued that the men with Eddred had been the ship's wizards.

"Sergeant!" Henry said.

The leader of the advance squad looked his way. "Sir?"

"Take your men and sweep that ship. Capture anyone still on board. Kill anyone that resists."

"Yes, sir. We have wounded."

"We'll tend to them. Hurry now."

The soldiers charged, weaving a random pattern to throw off any archers. They reached the end of the dock without a shot heading their way. Up the gangplank they went.

With nothing to do at the moment, Henry and his team got to work on the three soldiers that had taken arrows. All three had serious wounds, but none appeared fatal. The last wound was bound as the company sergeant returned from Eddred's ship.

"Not a soul on board, sir. They must have all jumped overboard."

"All right. Set a watch. Eddred has no other way out of the city. He'll make a run for his ship eventually. He has wizards with him, so we'll have to be extra careful."

With his trap set, it was only a matter of waiting for the prey to show up. Henry rubbed his hands together. If he captured Eddred and delivered him to Emperor Wolfric, he was sure to get a promotion out of his boring post.

There had been no sign of pursuit since they fled the palace gate which both pleased and confused Eddred. He fully expected to have dozens of Garenland soldiers hot on his trail, instead the back streets were practically deserted.

He paused in the alley between two stores and turned to Lilly. "Can you tell where they are?"

"No one's using the ether within my range. That suggests their wizards aren't searching for us. Beyond that I can't say. Should we turn back to the harbor?"

"I used a spell to render us invisible to their lookouts," Adam said. "Perhaps they lost track of us."

Heading back to the docks was exactly what they should do, but if the enemy wasn't chasing them, there was only one place they could be: the ship. He hoped the crew was safe but held out little hope. If they'd lost the ship, getting safely home was going to be a problem.

"I suppose we should take a look. We'll need to keep our distance lest we walk into a trap."

They set out, leaving the fine houses of the merchant district behind and approaching the rough warehouses of the docks. Curses filled the air as workers loaded and unloaded ships and wagons. Eddred and his guards walked calmly, trying to blend in. More people made it less likely they'd draw attention, especially since he doubted anyone in this part of the city would recognize him.

Just before the end of the last warehouse they stopped for a better look. Just as he'd feared, his ship was scarred by fire and a group of soldiers waited near the gangplank. The crew could be dead or captive for all he knew. Reclaiming his ship was out of the question as was escaping on their own. Maybe they could sneak out of the city after dark, but that was risky as well and got them no closer to Markane.

"Let's get out of here before someone notices us," Eddred said.

They retreated on a different line, trying to stay out of sight as much as possible. Eddred swallowed a sigh. What was he going to do now? Traveling to Lasil was certainly out of the question. He was so lost in thought he nearly didn't hear when someone said, "Majesty."

Lilly and Adam shifted to stand in front of him.

Before they could do anything, Captain Carter stepped out of the shadows of a closed-up tavern. His uniform was singed but otherwise he appeared unharmed. "I thought that was you, Your Majesty. Thank heaven you weren't captured."

"I was thinking the same thing, Carter." The two men shook hands. "What happened?"

"Those bastards took the ship. We tried to fight them off, but when the wizards started blasting, I ordered everyone over the side. We lost six sailors. Most of the lads are holed up not far from here in the storehouse of a friend of mine. Me and a few others were keeping watch for you."

"Good man. With you all safe, we've got enough hands to commandeer a boat."

"If we start something on the docks, the Garenlanders are bound to notice."

Eddred grinned. "That's why we're not going to try anything on the docks. We've got a few hours before the fishermen return. You, Lilly, and a handful of the boys are going to swim out and pretend you ran into trouble. When some kind-hearted soul stops to lend a hand, take his ship. We'll meet you two hundred yards east of the docks."

"Doesn't feel right, playing pirate," Carter said.

"Desperate times." Eddred put a hand on his shoulder. "You don't need to kill anyone, just toss them overboard. A little swim won't do any harm. If we're caught on the other hand..."

"Aye, my lord, no need to tell me. We'll get it done, never fear."

"I'm sure you will." Eddred said a silent prayer that they all survived.

Henry paced and muttered to himself. He'd been waiting for hours and still no sign of Eddred or any of the escaped sailors. Also no word from his spies in the city. If someone had seen them, Henry should have been informed. That was the problem when the other side had wizards too, you never knew exactly what they were capable of. Dusk was approaching and the city's fishing fleet was slowly returning to the harbor.

Maybe Eddred was going to try something in the dark. More likely he was going to stay hidden and force Henry to search the entire city. With his forces spread thin, it would be the perfect chance to try and escape. So many possibilities and so few facts.

He was just about to start another round of pacing when a blanket-wrapped man in the company of one of the soldiers he'd set to watch the perimeter approached. Henry broke off and marched right up to them.

Before he could get a word out the fellow in the blanket asked, "Are you in charge here? My boat was stolen."

Henry's heart sank. "Where and when?"

"Half a mile out not fifteen minutes ago. They looked like landsmen that flipped over their boat. Happens more than you might think. What do you think happens when I go to fish them out? Soon as they're aboard they pull daggers and put me and my crew over the side. Bloody lucky we could all swim."

"Which way did they go?" Henry asked.

"East and a little toward shore. Don't know what game they were playing. At that angle they'd miss the docks altogether. You going to get my boat back? She had a full catch too."

Henry ignored the request and shouted. "Two squads on me! The wizards as well. Move!"

The small force rushed west.

Fishermen and merchants alike hastened to move out of their way. Just as well since Henry would have happily killed anyone that slowed him even a step.

As he ran, he kept his eyes on the water. The boat had to be around here somewhere. At the very edge of the waterfront one of the wizards pointed and said, "There, sir, a sail."

Henry squinted and could just make out a white square against the sunset. "Can your spells reach them?"

The one who spoke raised a hand and quickly lowered it. "No, sir. Lord Shenk might have that sort of range, but we don't."

"Damn it! His Majesty isn't going to be pleased when he learns Eddred escaped." Henry just hoped the emperor punished him personally instead of leaving it to Lord Shenk. If there was one person in the world he didn't want mad at him, the young lord was it.

CHAPTER 38

A full day of rest and eating fine food had Otto feeling almost back to his old self. Not that he'd taken the whole day off. A quick visit to the warehouse assured him that everything ran smoothly in his absence. Sin reported nothing interesting happening and Otto got her busy searching for the wizards that had aided Cypher at the guild-hall. He doubted they were still in the city, but you couldn't be too careful.

Ulf seemed delighted to be working in his new lab and was having no trouble cranking out all the drugs they needed in Straken's mine. Axel had picked up the most recent batch himself. Otto would have liked to see him, but they could catch up anytime.

Hans and his squad were settled back in beside their armor and they'd fixed up a little cot for Corina as well. She spent so much time practicing that he had to warn her not to overdo it. Not that he was one to talk.

Satisfied that matters were as in hand as possible, Otto spent the rest of the day reading from one of the books he'd borrowed from the armory. It had been so long since he'd just taken a day for himself, he didn't quite know what to think, but it was nice.

All that said, when he received a summons to the palace this morning, he'd been happy to go. The messenger didn't give any details, only that Wolfric wanted to see him. This time they met in the throne room, though court was clear at the moment. The only other occupants were Wolfric and Borden.

Otto bowed to the throne and said, "You called for me, Majesty?"

"Yes, our agent in Lux has come with news. I wanted you here to listen firsthand. From his expression and fidgeting, I assume the news isn't good."

Otto silently kicked himself for not going to Lux when news of Eddred's arrival came in. Still, even if he escaped, there was little waiting for him back home, other than a lot of corpses, assuming Stephan's man did his job.

Wolfric nodded to Borden who stalked off only to return a moment later through one of the side doors with Henry in a firm grip. The spy fell to his knees. "I'm so sorry, Majesty. Eddred escaped us, though we did keep his ship."

Wolfric scowled but Otto spoke first, "Start at the beginning and tell us everything."

Henry did so. When he finished, he said, "I never imagined them swimming out to steal a fishing boat."

"Eddred is a nuisance, but a largely powerless one," Otto said. "Removing him would have been good, but his escape isn't the end of the world. What interests more is the conversation he had with Philippa."

"That interests me as well," Wolfric said.

"But she told me she told Eddred nothing." Henry looked from one to the other as if confused about why they cared.

"Of course she did," Wolfric said. "The question is was she lying or not. If she lied about helping him, I'll have to have her removed. Her head anyway."

"Shall we go question her?" Otto asked.

"Yes, we shall. Borden, prepare a security team. We're going to Lux."

~

As Otto emerged from the portal in Crystal City, Wolfric turned to him and said, "I must admit it feels good to get out of the castle. Some days I think dealing with the nobles and merchants drove Father mad before Straken had the chance. Perhaps we could do without them. Not Edwyn of course," he hastened to add.

Otto smiled. "I fear not, my friend. Boring as you find their reports, imagine how boring it would be to actually carry out all their duties. There wouldn't be enough hours in the day. Maybe you should give them more autonomy. As long as they pay their taxes on time and don't mistreat their people, who cares about the rest? I don't think my father went to the capital more than once every five or ten years."

"Not all the nobles share Arnwolf's strength of will. I suspect your father didn't come to court because he didn't want my father poking his nose into Shenk Barony's affairs."

"You might be right." The last of the guards emerged from the portal and Otto shut it down. All around them the portal guard was saluting their emperor.

Wolfric returned the gesture and waved. They hurried out of the fort and down the street toward the palace. It was a warm day and the air was heavy with humidity and salt. Three blocks from the portal Otto's tunic was soaked with sweat and he doubted the others were in any better shape.

"Perhaps we should have arranged a carriage," Otto said.

Wolfric laughed. "Nonsense, it feels good to walk. And who's going to complain if the emperor shows up a little sweaty. Ha! I'd like to see them try."

Otto couldn't argue with that. He kept the shield around them at full strength lest an archer try something foolish. It was exceedingly unlikely since no one knew they were coming, but Otto hadn't put this much effort into making Wolfric emperor only to lose him to carelessness.

They reached the palace gate without incident and the guards moved aside as they approached. Both men saluted as the emperor passed. The courtyard was empty and they were halfway across when the keep door opened and Philippa emerged with her honor guard around her.

Her smile was forced as she bowed to Wolfric. "A surprise visit, Majesty? How nice."

Wolfric waved her off. "This isn't a social call, Philippa. I understand you had another surprise visitor recently, an enemy of the Crown. Otto and I have come to discuss the matter."

She stiffened and flicked a venom-filled glance at Otto. "As I told your agent, he was looking for help against the empire and I told him I could do nothing."

"So I was informed. However, I'm not sure I trust your assurances. Otto's here to make sure. We'll need somewhere private to conduct the interview."

Her face twisted like she wanted to argue, but she clearly had no choice but to comply. From her reaction, Otto strongly suspected they were going to learn something unpleasant. At least unpleasant for her.

"If you insist. I have a private office we can use." She turned and they fell in behind her.

The inside of the Crystal Palace was beautifully lit by scores of Lux crystals. Crystal sculptures hung from the ceiling and sat on small tables here and there. It was unlike anything Otto had ever seen. It felt like anything he touched would break on the spot.

When they reached a particular door Philippa said, "Through here."

"No one in or out, Borden," Wolfric said. "We shouldn't be long."

Philippa's private office was more practical than Otto had expected. There was a large desk, chairs, a carafe and glasses. She went behind her desk and sat facing them.

Otto closed the door. There was a sound behind him and when he turned, he found Philippa holding a hand crossbow and pointing it right at Wolfric's chest. A meaningless gesture since he was protected by Otto's magic.

"I suppose questions won't be necessary after all," Wolfric said. "Being governor wasn't enough for you?"

"It's an insult. But you knew that when you offered me the job."

"Then why accept? You had a hope of ever being even a minor inconvenience to us."

"I'm leaving," Philippa said. "Make a sound and I'll kill you. Understand?"

"Perfectly," Wolfric said.

Otto tapped his ring and sent a thread of ether out, binding her where she stood. He walked over and removed the bolt from her crossbow.

"You can't possibly have imagined that would work." Wolfric backhanded her across the face. "Tomorrow you hang like a common criminal. Something I should have done from the start. Borden!"

The office door opened and Borden asked, "Majesty?"

"Take the former governor into custody. We'll be hanging her in the city square tomorrow. Arrange to have a scaffold built. Nothing fancy."

"Yes, Majesty."

Borden took Philippa by the arm and Otto released his spell. He dragged her out, leaving Otto and Wolfric alone.

"I didn't think she had it in her," Wolfric said.

"How does the saying go, a cornered animal is the most dangerous? She must have conspired with Eddred and known we'd find out. Just as well we dealt with her now before she did any real harm."

"I suppose."

"I thought you'd be pleased." Otto cocked his head. "Weren't you looking for an excuse to deal with her after she betrayed your father's trust?"

"Yes, but now that it's happened, I feel... empty. I know everything we've done was necessary for Garenland's safety, but it's not as thrilling as I'd first hoped. Is it strange that I'm already bored with being an emperor?"

Otto hated it when Wolfric acted like the noble he was. Bored with being the most powerful man in the empire. If the other nations had had their way, he'd be as dead as Philippa soon would be. He couldn't say any of that to Wolfric of course. A bit of soothing was in order.

"Maybe the nobles are right," Otto said. "A wife and family might be what you really need. Something to take your mind off the day-to-day drudgery of rulership."

"A wife doesn't appeal to me at the moment, but I've read

that emperors often kept a harem. That might make a good distraction."

Otto grinned. "Indeed, it might. And I know just the person to provide you with beautiful, and properly vetted, companions. I'll look into it as soon as we finish here."

Wolfric's glum face perked up at the prospect. Otto felt certain Sin could find just the right sort of women for him.

CHAPTER 39

The only good thing Eddred had noticed about being stuck on a loaded fishing sloop with thirty sailors was they didn't lack for food. That said, when Markane Harbor came into view he breathed a long sigh of relief. He needed a bath and some real food and he needed them badly.

He squinted into the glare, trying to make out details. Something seemed wrong. There were no people moving around. This time of day the docks should have been bustling.

"Begging your pardon, Majesty," Captain Carter said. "But with our ship still in Lux, what are me and the men supposed to do?"

Technically the royal flagship was Eddred's, but he knew what Carter meant. "Don't worry, we'll find something for you. Though I may have to break up the crew and divide them among other ships."

The men grumbled and Eddred didn't blame them. Most of them had been serving on his ship for years. It would take time for them to fit in with a new crew, but under the circumstances he didn't know what else could be done.

When they passed the outer barrier the sailor on lookout said, "Is that Lord Valtan standing on the boardwalk?"

Eddred scrambled across the dead, stinking fish and focused where he pointed. That was Valtan. What in heaven's name was he doing?

His thoughts were interrupted by an overwhelming force lifting the ship and turning them ninety degrees to run parallel to the dock.

"What was that?" Carter asked as he fought the tiller.

"Valtan. He doesn't want us to dock." What Eddred couldn't understand was why.

"Eddred, can you hear me?" Valtan's disembodied voice boomed across the deck.

"I can. Why did you stop us?"

"The city has been cursed. Everyone on the main island is dead and anyone that sets foot on it will quickly join them."

Eddred's heart lurched. Nearly fifty thousand people lived on the main island including his wife. Around him the sailors were cursing and, in a few cases, crying. Eddred didn't blame them a bit.

When Eddred finally got himself somewhat under control he asked, "How?"

"An artifact created by one of my former comrades. Someone, I assume one of the raiders from Garenland though I have no proof, put it in one of the city wells. From there the curse traveled through the aquifer all over the island. The only saving grace is that the barrier islands aren't connected so the people there are safe."

That was a small comfort, but it was something. "What happens now?"

"How did you make out with Philippa?" Valtan asked. "I assume poorly if you've returned without your ship."

"The meeting went fine, but the Garenland garrison seized my ship and nearly captured us. Philippa said she'd do what she could, which is little more than share any information she might pick up. I don't dare try my luck in Lasil, or anywhere else on the continent for that matter. I'm on Wolfric's hit list and word will have spread to keep their eyes open."

"I fear we must accept the fact that for now at least, the war is lost." The weariness came through loud and clear in Valtan's voice. "The only hope we have of reclaiming what we've lost is to bring in outside help."

"And where would we find anyone powerful and crazy enough to help us with an invasion?"

"To the west, the people of Colt's Nation might be willing to lend a hand, assuming you can convince them that Garenland will be turning its sights their way if they don't. If they agree they'll have to sail here."

Eddred shook his head even though he doubted Valtan could see. "Suppose we survive the crossing, why would they believe me about Garenland? They're a long way away and not connected to the portal network. An attack on their country would takes years to plan and execute."

"They might not believe you, but they're our best bet. If negotiations fail, we can regroup and pursue other options. If you have any suggestions, I'm perfectly willing to listen."

That might well be the first time Valtan had asked his opinion on anything. It spoke to just how desperate their situation was. "I'll go, but we can't make the trip in this little ship and we'll need supplies."

"Any food from the city will be tainted by the curse. You'll have to make a detour to the City of Coins to buy supplies.

Money at least I can give you without fear. Oh, and you'll need to stop at South Barrier Island and pick up Uther. Somehow he survived both the curse and the raiders. I've spoken to him, so he'll be ready."

Eddred and his shipmates spent several hours in silence, each trying to come to grips with the situation. Every man had lost someone, most lost their entire family. Eddred didn't begin to have the words to console them. In fact, it was taking everything he had to keep from breaking down himself.

When Valtan returned, one of the big, two-masted trading ships began to move on its own. The huge vessel slid out beside them and Valtan said, "This should serve you well. I've purified the ship and placed several chests of gold inside. I wish you the best of luck."

A rope ladder appeared from the ship's deck and the sailors began climbing.

"What about you?" Eddred asked. "You have nothing to eat or drink."

Valtan's laugh was bitter. "I need neither. I'm immortal, remember. I think this curse is Otto Shenk's way of punishing me for daring to resist his plans. Some of this is my fault, I accept that, but even so I could have done nothing differently."

"It's not your fault, it's Garenland's fault, and we'll make them pay for what they did, somehow."

"Hold your spirit tight, Eddred, I fear you will have need of it before this matter is done."

Eddred didn't doubt that for a second. He was the last man out of the fishing boat. At the helm the captain asked, "What course, Majesty?"

"To South Barrier Island then on to the City of Coins."

CHAPTER 40

Otto was waiting on the docks when Captain Wainwright brought his ship in. He'd been spending more time in Lux since the former queen's execution. There had been some complaints, little of it overt, but for the most part, the people seemed to accept that their queen's mistake wouldn't damage their lives. So when a week passed and the garrison didn't hang anyone else, people returned to their normal lives. That was the best reaction Otto could have hoped for.

He stepped back to make room for the sailors hustling to tie the ship up. The gangplank fell into place and Stephan strode down. His hairline had retreated a little further, but otherwise he appeared in good health. His scowl, on the other hand, indicated less than goodwill.

"Welcome back," Otto said. "I trust your mission went smoothly."

"Smooth enough, though the loot was meager."

"The loot was always going to be meager. You were raiding

farms and tiny villages. I assumed it was the entertainment value that convinced you to come."

Stephan's smile was twisted and dark. "We had great fun. Though once your magical trinket killed everyone on the main island, the men lost much of their enthusiasm. I decided it was time to return home."

Otto took a moment to process what his brother just said. The skull was only supposed to wipe out the city, not the surrounding towns. "Are you certain it killed everyone?"

"So Julian said." Stephan jerked a thumb over his shoulder. "Ask him yourself."

Otto intended to do exactly that, but he had one more matter to discuss with Stephan. "If you can spare a few days, I've got a special bonus for all your hard work."

"What sort of bonus?" He couldn't have sounded more dubious.

"I don't want to spoil the surprise, but I'm confident you'll enjoy it. Interested?"

"Sure, I'm in no rush to get back to Griswalda and Father."

"Good. I'll speak to Julian and Captain Wainwright, then we can leave."

Otto left his brother and went up on deck. He followed the ether to Julian, or more accurately the ring he'd lent the man, and found him huddled and trembling near the main mast.

"I understand you carried out your mission well." Otto crouched so he was at eye level. "Congratulations. I need the ring back now."

Julian's wide, frightened eyes locked on to him. "I'll die without it."

Otto shook his head. "You're safe now. The curse can't reach you across the ocean. You have gold enough to retire and live in comfort. The emperor and I both extend our thanks for your hard work."

"I killed them all. I found bodies all the way to the bridge. They were lying everywhere."

"What about animals?" Otto asked.

Julian cocked his head. "Animals? I didn't see any. Didn't hear any either. Did I kill them too?"

That was a distinct possibility, but Otto saw no value in pointing it out. "You did your duty like a good soldier should."

Otto held out his hand and Julian slowly pulled the white ring off his finger. The bone circle felt cold to the touch, but Otto ignored it. He helped Julian to his feet and guided him toward the gangplank.

Poor bastard. Otto wouldn't be surprised to hear about a suicide in the near future.

Captain Wainwright was standing by the wheel and Otto joined him there. "Lord Shenk. I didn't expect to see you here. Is all well?"

Otto nodded. All was surprisingly well. "Anything interesting to report?"

"Just one thing. I can't say if it means anything or not, but we passed a ship sailing due west. It was a Markane ship, but it made no move to engage us. Given their head start I had no hope of catching them, but I thought it interesting."

Otto agreed. It had to be Eddred since everyone else on the island was dead, but what was he up to? Maybe his master would have an idea. He needed to speak with her soon anyway.

"I may need to give chase. Would you be interested in another government contract?"

"Be my pleasure. When do we sail?"

"No idea but be ready. When I arrive I'll want to leave

quickly. You can keep Garenland's share of the loot as payment."

"Then we are at your service, my lord."

Otto left him, his mind racing. Whatever Eddred was planning, it couldn't be good for the empire. He found Stephan giving his men orders a little way away from the ship.

"They'll meet us in Garen with Shenk Barony's cut of the loot," Stephan said. "Now what's this about a bonus?"

<hr />

"What the bloody hell is that?" Stephan stared at the tower that served as the Wizards Guild's secret base.

Otto couldn't help smiling at his brother's reaction. They'd been traveling for the past three days to get here. First taking the portal from Lux to Rolan then by horse across the plains. Otto could have traveled through the ether by himself, but then he couldn't have brought Stephan and that was the whole point.

"That is where the Wizards Guild hid for many years. They kidnapped me, dragged me here, and tried to use magic to compel me to join their cause. They failed and all but two of them are either dead or captured."

"Fascinating, but what has that got to do with me?"

"Enoch joined them and betrayed me in the process. He's locked in a cell right now. I thought you might like an hour or two alone with him."

Stephan shot him a look. "How long have you known where he was?"

"Since last summer. He was useful until he decided his loyalty lay elsewhere. And stop glaring at me like that. There are more important things than your petty revenge."

"Then why indulge me now?"

"Because now I have the time and desire to see my former teacher suffer. You being an expert in that field, I couldn't think of anyone better suited to the job, or anyone that would enjoy it more. If I was wrong, we can turn back."

"You weren't wrong."

Otto kept his expression neutral, but he was smiling on the inside. He'd known perfectly well that he was right. He couldn't wait to see the look on his faithless master's face when he saw Stephan.

As they approached the tower door, a pair of wizards he'd left on guard duty appeared as if out of nowhere. They both saluted.

"Any news?" Otto asked.

"All quiet here, Lord Shenk."

"Good. If the guild had any intention of returning to rescue their friends, they'd have done it by now. I'll be sealing the tower when we're finished. I know this was a boring job so thank you for your diligence."

They saluted again and Otto dismounted along with Stephan. Inside, Otto led the way downstairs to the holding cells. The long hall was empty. Otto turned to Stephan. "Wait here a moment."

Otto continued on alone. He found the three cages pretty much as he left them plus a lingering stink of waste and body odor. All three prisoners scrambled to their feet when he entered.

He ignored Tal and Esmay and stopped directly in front of Enoch. "It seems your friends aren't coming back for you. Was betraying me worth it?"

"I only did what I thought best for all wizards," Enoch said. "Please, Otto, let me out of here. I'll continue to serve you to the best of my ability. Can't you forgive me, for old times' sake?"

"No. And I certainly can't trust you to continue training the war wizards. Heaven only knows what foolishness you've already stuck in their heads. This is where we part ways, forever. Stephan!"

Stephan strode down the hallway and stopped beside Otto. "I told you I'd see you again, old man."

"Please, kill me if you must, but don't let this brute do it."

"Despite our differences, I find working with my brother both straightforward and beneficial. He's done good service for the empire. It's only fair that he gets a proper reward." Otto took the key out of his satchel and unlocked the door.

"What about us?" Tal demanded.

Otto turned to the big man. "I'll have you executed as soon as my brother is finished. Holler when you're done, Stephan."

"What about his magic?" Stephan asked before Otto could leave.

"He can't use it in that cell. How else do you think they could have held me for so long? Have fun, brother."

Stephan entered Enoch's cell and Otto locked it behind him before returning to the first floor. He needed to figure out how to reset the tower's magical protections before they left. He'd also need to collect the others on guard duty.

The first pained scream drifted up to him. Given Stephan's proclivities, he should have plenty of time.

CHAPTER 41

Otto appeared in his master's tower and found it exactly as he remembered. In a world of nonstop change, it was the one constant. The single second-floor chamber held only the enchanted mirror through which Lord Karonin interacted with the world. Her green tinged but still attractive face appeared surrounded by a halo of dark, floating hair.

"Master." Otto bowed.

"It has been some time, Apprentice. I trust you have progress to report."

"Much, Master. The continent is now under Garenland's rule and wizards are free to live everywhere as full citizens. Aside from a few minor irritants, no one remains to question our rule."

"Not your rule. Do you still refuse to seize direct power?" Her disapproval stung, but Otto had no desire to sit around like Wolfric day in and day out and give orders.

"The people wouldn't accept a wizard as emperor. Better

for everyone if I remain behind the scenes. It also frees me up to continue my training."

Lord Karonin's smile was as sharp as a razor. "You want to know about the next step in becoming an Arcane Lord."

"Yes, Master. I believe I have met your conditions. I also have some questions. I spoke to Valtan—"

"When? How? He is a liar and a coward. You can trust no word he tells you."

Otto winced at her fury. She really did hate the man. "It wasn't my choice. I was traveling through the ether near Markane City and he dragged me to him. He claims that when I broke through my personal barrier, that I replaced a portion of my soul with ether and that it has made me less human. Is that true?"

"Yes." Her direct response surprised him. "The only way you can grow past a certain point is to get rid of the parts that hold you back. Humans are weak, pathetic creatures. You are already well beyond them and the better for it. Once you become an Arcane Lord, all your weaknesses will be gone and the ether will be yours to do with as you please. That's what you want, is it not?"

Was it? Otto couldn't help thinking about Valtan's warning and combining it with everything he'd noticed of his own changes in personality. Then again, leaving his humanity and its endless disappointment behind could only be a relief.

"It is," he said at last. "My other question was about what lies to the west across the ocean. One of my enemies, a pawn of Valtan's, was seen sailing that way. Is there something he could find that might be a threat to us?"

"Colt's Nation is to the west. We had some trade, but he and I never saw eye to eye. He organized his people into ten city-states. Whether they would be willing to help your enemy isn't something I can answer, but if they do, you will face a powerful enemy. Colt specialized in what he called magical engineering, creating devices like the enchanted armor you took from my armory."

"Maybe I should follow him. I can speak to them and explain that Garenland has no desire for war."

"That is a good idea. Your next step on the journey to becoming an Arcane Lord lies through Colt's workshop. He kept one of the three pieces of the Immortality Engine. If you are to complete the transformation you must recover that piece."

Otto's heart raced. "What is it called?"

"The Chamber of Eternity. It's made of magical glass and serves as the central component of the engine. It's big enough for a single person to stand within and has a trio of mithril rods at the top which hold the second component, the Heart of Alchemy. You'll have no trouble spotting it as I doubt there is anything similar anywhere in the world."

"I will make preparations to depart as soon as possible."

"Good. Once you've completed the transformation, you can kill the pig Valtan."

"About him. I have already begun his punishment."

"What do you mean?" She sounded so suspicious. Did she truly trust him so little?

Otto told her about the skull and killing everyone on the island. "He is alone surrounded by the dead. It seems almost a worse fate than death. Plus, keeping him alive allows for his continued use as a power source."

His master's laugh was cold and humorless. "That is wonderful. I knew making you my apprentice was a wise course. You will make a fine Arcane Lord."

Otto nodded, less pleased than he would have been a

month ago. But his course was set now and he would succeed, no matter how many bodies lay behind him.

AUTHOR NOTE

Hello everyone and thank you very much for reading The Master of Magic. I hope you've enjoyed Otto's story so far, dark though it might have been.

His quest for the power of an Arcane Lord continues in book 5, The Chamber of Eternity. I hope you'll join me for that one as well.

Until next time, thanks for reading,

James

ALSO BY JAMES E WISHER

The Portal Wars Saga

The Hidden Tower

The Great Northern War

The Portal Thieves

The Master of Magic

The Dragonspire Chronicles

The Black Egg

The Mysterious Coin

The Dragons' Graveyard

The Slave War

The Sunken Tower

The Dragon Empress

The Dragonspire Chronicles Omnibus Vol. 1

The Dragonspire Chronicles Omnibus Vol. 2

The Complete Dragonspire Chronicles Omnibus

Soul Force Saga

Disciples of the Horned One Trilogy:

Darkness Rising

Raging Sea and Trembling Earth

Harvest of Souls

Disciples of the Horned One Omnibus

ABOUT THE AUTHOR

James E. Wisher is a writer of science fiction and fantasy novels. He's been writing since high school and reading everything he could get his hands on for as long as he can remember.

To learn more:
www.jamesewisher.com
james@jamesewisher.com

Printed in the USA
CPSIA information can be obtained
at www.ICGtesting.com
LVHW041727240124
769628LV00002B/260